"You really gave the only proof of your innocence to your younger brother?" Jake asked. And he didn't bother hiding his skepticism.

Lillian flinched. "I know you don't think much of my family."

"They break the law," he reminded her. And despite her claims of innocence, she might have broken the law, as well.

She flinched again. "Not Donny. He's a good kid."

"He's still a Davies."

"So am I," she said. Then she rubbed her palms over her belly. "So is this baby..."

His baby?

He needed to know. But he wasn't certain he could believe anything she told him. If that flash drive existed, though, if she was telling the truth about that...

Maybe he could trust her again, like he had all those months ago when he'd started falling for her.

* * *

Be sure to check out the previous books in the exciting Top Secret Deliveries miniseries.

* * *

If you're on Twitter, tell us what you think of Harlequin Romantic Suspense! #harlequinromsuspense

Dear Reader,

I am so excited to have my book, *The Bounty Hunter's Baby Surprise*, included in Harlequin Romantic Suspense's Top Secret Deliveries series! I do adore babies. The only ones I've been around recently have belonged to other people, though.

But I do remember that feeling of being pregnant and I'm not talking about just the surge of hormones that made me weep over coffee commercials. I'm talking about that feeling of protectiveness. I would have done anything for my babies even before they were born. That's how I can relate to Lillian Davies, the heroine in *The Bounty Hunter's Baby Surprise*. She will go to any extremes to protect her baby—even running from trumped-up charges against her and the bounty hunter determined to make her face those charges. But Jake Howard has never not collected a bounty. He has returned every bail jumper he's ever chased. But he gets more than he bargained for when he tracks down Lillian Davies.

I hope you enjoy this story as much as I enjoyed writing it.

Happy reading!

Lisa Childs

THE BOUNTY HUNTER'S BABY SURPRISE

Lisa Childs

HARLEQUIN®ROMANTIC SUSPENSE

Recycling programs
for this product may
not exist in your area.

ISBN-13: 978-1-335-45643-4

The Bounty Hunter's Baby Surprise

Copyright © 2018 by Lisa Childs

HARLEQUIN®
www.Harlequin.com

Printed in U.S.A.

Ever since **Lisa Childs** read her first romance novel (a Harlequin story, of course) at age eleven, all she wanted was to be a romance writer. With over forty novels published with Harlequin, Lisa is living her dream. She is an award-winning, bestselling romance author. Lisa loves to hear from readers, who can contact her on Facebook, through her website, lisachilds.com, or her snail-mail address, PO Box 139, Marne, MI 49435.

Books by Lisa Childs

Harlequin Romantic Suspense

Top Secret Deliveries

The Bounty Hunter's Baby Surprise

Bachelor Bodyguards

His Christmas Assignment
Bodyguard Daddy
Bodyguard's Baby Surprise
Beauty and the Bodyguard
Nanny Bodyguard
Single Mom's Bodyguard
In the Bodyguard's Arms

The Coltons of Shadow Creek

The Colton Marine

Visit the Author Profile page at Harlequin.com for more titles.

With great appreciation for Patience Bloom;
it is a privilege and a joy to work with you!

Prologue

Pulling the flash drive from the computer with trembling fingers, Lillian Davies ducked under the desk just as the office door creaked open to the corridor. A beam of light flashed across the space, bouncing off the filing cabinets and the back of the chair she'd pulled up against the desk to cover her. She closed her eyes so the beam would not glint in them, and she crouched even lower. Her heart pounded wildly with fear that she would be caught.

If that happened, she would never have a chance to show anyone the evidence that would clear her name. And she would be sent to prison for certain. She held her breath, waiting to be discovered.

If the security guard noticed that the monitor was on…

She could only hope that he would call the police.

Because if he called his boss—her former boss—first...

Then she might not make it back to jail. He would undoubtedly kill to cover up his crime—the one for which he'd framed her. Tom Kuipers must have hired her so he would have a scapegoat for the blame. She'd thought he was one of the few people in River City, Michigan, who hadn't judged her based on her last name and who her family was and had been giving her a chance to prove herself.

But she had been wrong. Again.

Tears stung her eyes. She should have been used to it, used to being used. She blinked back the tears, opened her eyes and lifted her chin.

No. She damn well was not going to get used to it. She was going to fight back this time. Because she wasn't fighting just for herself anymore.

And if the security guard discovered her, she would fight him, too. Sure, he carried a gun. But he wouldn't actually shoot her, would he? Maybe if she propelled the chair into his legs and knocked him over she would have a chance to run for it.

She locked the trembling fingers of her free hand around the legs of the chair, ready to use it as a weapon. But the beam shut off, plunging the office into darkness again, except for the faint glow from the parking lot lights outside the windows. Then the door creaked closed and snapped shut.

Lillian finally released the breath she'd been holding. She waited several more moments, though, before she pushed out the chair and crawled out of her hiding space. She opened her purse and dropped the flash drive inside it. The plastic device slid to the bottom where she'd dropped the pregnancy test. She'd enclosed that in a bag, and through the clear plastic she could see the results that she hadn't waited to read.

She already knew she was pregnant. She'd never missed one month let alone two, going on three. The plus sign staring up at her confirmed it, though. That was why she had risked her life and her freedom to come back here. She needed the evidence to prove her innocence, so that yet another Davies didn't wind up in prison.

If the flash drive didn't get the charges dropped against her, she was going to run. She was not going to have her baby behind bars. It was bad enough that was where most of the Davies family wound up later in life; her child was not going to begin his or her life in jail.

Chapter 1

Six months later...

"I should have listened to you," Seymour Tuttle said. The bail bondsman paced the small confines of his office, nearly tripping over Jake Howard's feet as the little man made the pass between his desk and the door Jake was leaning his back against, his long legs crossed at the ankles.

Tuttle had called him into his office and told him to shut the door. That was never a good sign for Jake. Every time someone had spoken to him in private before, it had been to give him bad news.

Your mother is dead...

Your father is gone...

But usually Tuttle didn't give a damn about privacy—his or anyone else's. But since he'd just admitted he was wrong, Jake understood his not wanting anyone else to overhear his admission. He was surprised the stubborn old guy had admitted it even to himself, let alone Jake. That must have been Tuttle's version of bad news: being wrong.

"What should you have listened to me about?" Jake asked, holding back his "I told you so" until he knew the specifics.

"The Davies family." Tuttle uttered the last name as if it was a vulgar curse word.

Jake flinched at just the mention of it, and a twinge of pain clenched his heart, stealing away his breath and his words. He couldn't speak.

But Tuttle didn't stop talking. He rarely did. His wide mouth was nearly as big as his short body. "You told me not to bail out another one of them." He shook his little bald head in self-disgust. "You warned me that they always run."

Jake's pulse was running now in overtime. He didn't want to think about the Davies family, didn't want to think about what he'd done, the extremes he'd gone to the last time that he'd had to apprehend two of them.

"Why aren't you saying it?" Tuttle demanded as he stopped in front of him.

Jake blinked and stared down at the little man. Tuttle was barely five feet tall to Jake's well over six-foot height. "Saying what?"

"I told you so," Tuttle said. "You were right. I paid the bail and now you need to go bring back another damn Davies for me."

Jake shook his head and ran a slightly shaking hand through his thick hair. He needed a haircut. But then he always needed a haircut. "Not me. That's *not* going to happen."

"You're the expert on the Davies family," Tuttle persisted. "You know where to find them."

"In jail," Jake said. "That's where most of them are." He couldn't believe Don or Dave would have gotten bail again after jumping it last time. And if a judge had been stupid enough to give it to them, Seymour had been even stupider to pay it. "I told you so" wasn't enough recrimination for risking his money on one of them again.

"Not her," Seymour said.

And Jake's blood froze in his veins, sending a chill straight to his soul. "What?"

Tuttle paced around his desk, pulled out his chair and plopped down onto it. The metal desk was old and scratched up. His leather chair was more duct tape than leather. The bail bondsman liked money, but he didn't like spending it. Leafing through a sheaf of papers on his desk, he held up a mug shot. "Her. I thought she was different than the rest of them. She has no record. No prior arrests at all. That's the only reason the judge granted her bail. That's why I posted it, even though I know you warned me not to."

He trailed off as if waiting for Jake to say something—anything—but Jake was too stunned. He couldn't move as shock gripped him. Seymour couldn't be talking about...

Not Lillian.

But she was the only female Davies now. Her mother had passed away when Lillian was eighteen, leaving her with her degenerate father, three older brothers and one younger one.

"Her trial was supposed to start Monday," Seymour said, "but she never showed up for court."

Trial. For what? What the hell was going on?

Jake's spine stiffened. He shot away from the door to grab the mug shot from Tuttle's hand. As he stared down at the photo, myriad emotions passed through him.

Guilt. He'd felt that for the past eight months every time he had thought of her, which had been always. She had never left his mind. He remembered how devastated she had looked that last time he'd seen her, how her beautiful blue eyes had been dark with betrayal and pain. She'd thought he'd used her. And he had. That had been his plan all along, to get close to her to find out where her dad and brother Dave were hiding, but then something else had happened to him.

Desire. He hadn't planned on that, hadn't plotted to get as close to her as he had gotten. But he'd wanted Lillian Davies more than he'd ever wanted any woman. With her shimmery pale blond hair and deep blue eyes, she was stunningly beautiful. And sweet. She had acted and tasted so damn sweet. Her kisses had gone straight to his head and desire had gone to his groin. He hadn't been able to resist her. And he'd nearly forgotten all about apprehending her dad and eldest brother.

Maybe that had been her plan, though. Maybe she had known all along who he really was and she'd set out to seduce him into forgetting about the bounties on her brother and father.

Anger. He felt it now as he stared down at her mug shot. He could barely look at her beautiful face, and she was still beautiful—even with dark circles rimming her eyes. He looked instead at the charge printed on the photo: embezzlement. She must have played him, just like she had everyone else. Her boss, the judge and the bail bondsman. Lily-white Lillian Davies was anything but. She was a con artist just like the rest of her criminal family.

"I know, I know," Tuttle said. "You told me that if I bailed one of them out again, that you didn't want to hear about it, that you wanted nothing to do with any of them again. But…"

Jake had been adamant about that because he hadn't thought he'd ever be able to face her again—because he'd felt so damn guilty over hurting her.

He'd staged their whole *cute* first meeting, literally bumping into her in the grocery store. She'd apologized when their carts had collided, even though he'd deliberately plowed his into hers. Somehow he had sweet-talked her into dinner and then he'd made it for her.

All he had been after was information on her dad and brother Dave. But he'd gotten so much more…

Had he seduced her, though? Or had it been the other way around?

"I'll call one of the O'Hanigans to bring her in instead," Tuttle offered.

"No!" was Jake's sharp retort as some emotion even uglier than anger coursed through him. Was it jealousy? He'd never felt such a sick, twisty feeling in his stomach before. He didn't want Lillian seducing one of the O'Hanigans like she'd seduced him.

No, if she was going to seduce anyone…

Images flitted through his mind, like they did every night when he tried to sleep. Images of her lying naked in his bed, her silky skin flushed with desire, her lips parted on a husky moan.

No. She wasn't going to seduce him this time. He would not be conned twice. He'd spent the past eight months hating himself for making her hate him. He'd felt guilty and remorseful because he'd hurt her.

And she'd probably been laughing at him—as she stole money just like her brother and father had. She'd been laughing at him and her hapless trusting employer.

She wasn't going to get away with it.

Not this time.

She wasn't going to elude justice.

This was why he had resigned from the US Marshals and gone into business for himself as a bounty hunter. The US Marshals didn't have the time or the resources to bring back all the fugitives from justice. So Jake had taken it upon himself to do the job.

"Don't call the O'Hanigans," he said with more control. "*I* will bring back Lillian Davies." He'd spent the past eight months dreading ever seeing her again, but now he couldn't wait.

His pulse tripping away with anticipation, he turned toward the door but not so fast that he missed the little smile that curved Seymour Tuttle's thin lips. The old bail bondsman had played him—just like Lillian had.

He would deal with Tuttle later. Right now, he had a fugitive to apprehend. A beautiful fugitive...

Lillian felt sicker than she had during her first trimester when she hadn't just had morning sickness but all-day sickness. Of course, that might have had less to do with her pregnancy than the charges she faced—charges that could put her behind bars for a very long time.

But jail was the least of her concerns at the moment.

Her heart pounded fast and her palms sweated against the steering wheel she clutched. She had no idea where to go now. Since ditching court, she was a fugitive.

She knew what that meant. She knew *who* might come looking for her. That was her biggest concern, even bigger than finding out what the hell had happened to the flash drive.

Her lawyer claimed she'd never received it. But dare Lillian believe her?

Or had *he* gotten to her? Her former boss.

Mr. Kuipers was wealthy, even wealthier since he'd embezzled all that money from his company. He could have easily bribed an underpaid legal aid attorney to lose the evidence that would have proved Lillian's innocence and his guilt.

That had to be what happened. She couldn't consider the alternative. Then it would only prove that Jake Howard had been right about her family.

And he wasn't...

He hadn't been right about anything. But the man was good at his job—so good that he would use whatever means necessary to get what he wanted. Just like he had used her.

She hadn't been complaining at the time, though. Of course, she had been totally unaware that he was using her. She'd been so naive.

Again. Why did she trust people that she shouldn't?

But Jake had overwhelmed her—with his good

looks, his charm. Her pulse quickened just thinking about him, how he'd looked at her that first time he'd literally bumped into her. His dark eyes had twinkled with amusement, and his sexy lips had curved into that wicked grin of his. He was so damn good-looking with those chiseled features and overly long thick dark hair. And his body.

Tall, broad and muscular.

And powerful.

While she was naive, Lillian had never been romantic or foolish. She'd never believed in love at first sight—until that moment. But it had been like she'd always known Jake and he her.

Of course she had—she just hadn't realized it at the time, especially since he'd given her a different name. He'd called himself Jacob Williams. If he'd told her Jake Howard, she would have recognized him as the ruthless bounty hunter her family feared. She had felt a flicker of fear at that first meeting—because she'd somehow instinctively known her life was about to change forever.

Her baby kicked her belly, and she moved her hand from the steering wheel to rub over the bump where a little foot pushed against her abdomen. "Shh…"

She needed to calm down; she couldn't risk her anxiety causing any harm to her baby. She had to think.

Where could she go?

If Jake came looking for her, he was bound to figure out where she was hiding. But he wouldn't come, would he? After what he'd done, how he'd deceived and hurt her, he couldn't have the guts to ever face her again.

That was what she was counting on…

She'd also been counting on that flash drive clearing her of all charges, though. And now the flash drive was gone. What the hell was she going to do?

Should she break into the lawyer's office and look for it? She stared up at the dark building and considered it. What would breaking and entering charges add to her embezzlement sentence? Too long to risk it.

She had to think of something else. But first, she needed some rest. Because she didn't trust Mr. Kuipers, she'd ignored the judge and the bail bondsman's order to not leave the state, and she'd gone to Florida and the place her grandmother owned but hadn't been able to use this winter. To get back in time for the court date in River City, Michigan, Lillian had driven all night.

If only she'd called her lawyer before she'd made the trip…

But she'd waited until she'd been back in Michigan only to be told that the flash drive had never arrived. The lawyer had to be lying. Lillian refused to consider that another person she'd trusted had let her down.

She blinked back the tears stinging her eyes and focused on the street in front of her. She wasn't far from her apartment, but she'd given that up six months ago, right after she'd been bailed out of jail.

She should have given up the place sooner. All it had done was remind her of Jake, of how he'd cooked for her the first time they'd met, bumping into each other in the tiny kitchen, bodies brushing against bodies, that awareness making her tingle everywhere…

It had reminded her of how he'd grinned at her, his

dark eyes sparkling with amusement. She'd thought he was the one man who appreciated her goofy sense of humor. But he'd probably only been amused because he was making a fool of her for falling for him when he was just using her.

And because of how he'd used her, she would always have a reminder of him now. She rubbed her hand over her belly again, and the baby moved beneath her touch.

His baby.

But she didn't want him to know that, not after how he'd treated her. She didn't want their child to have a father like him—one so ruthless and uncaring.

He couldn't find her.

Nobody could.

"I want her dead!" Tom Kuipers shouted the words at the men gathered before him. Some of them flinched. A couple of them looked away from him.

They might be appalled at his ruthlessness, but they wouldn't turn on him. Unlike Lillian Davies, they knew what happened to people who crossed him. They were never able to cross anyone again.

He raised his picture of Lillian Davies, blown up from her employee ID badge, and waved it at the group of seven or eight men gathered in the middle of the warehouse between the rows of building equipment and supplies. It was after hours. No one would overhear this meeting. And no one would repeat the contents of it.

He trusted these men because he knew they feared him. He wasn't a large man or particularly muscular, and at fifty-six, he was no longer as young as he'd once been. But he was so much more powerful than he'd ever been. And they all knew it.

"She might have altered her appearance." If she was smart.

And Lillian Davies was actually smarter than he'd realized. He'd thought she was so ignorant and trusting. And he had counted on her unsuspecting nature when he'd set her up to take the fall for all that money going missing.

But she wasn't tumbling down as easily as he'd thought. Instead of showing up in court for the trial that would have sentenced her to prison, she was fighting back.

And he could not tolerate that.

"Whoever kills her and provides me with proof of her death will get a huge bonus for their loyalty," he promised. It was, like so many others, a promise on which he would probably renege.

Tom had already spent more of that money he'd stolen than he'd wanted to. He had plans for it, plans for a new life.

But they didn't know he was lying. Just like Lillian once had, they trusted his word.

"Do you have any idea where she is?" one of the men asked him.

He glared at the idiot. "If I knew, she'd already be dead." He would have taken immense pleasure in doing it himself for all the trouble she'd caused him. Not only had she not taken the fall for which he'd set her up, but she'd recently tried to extort money from him, too.

Did that damn flash drive even really exist?

Once she was found, he would have her searched for it, just in case.

But first, she had to be found. Then she and the flash drive would both be destroyed.

Lillian Davies could not hide forever.

Chapter 2

Jake leaned against the door frame as the elderly woman foraged around her living room. He could barely see over her boxes and stacks of magazines and plastic totes that were so full the lids wouldn't even snap into place. One day he would probably see her apartment again—on the news or on an episode of *Hoarders*.

"I know I left her box over here," she murmured from behind one of the stacks. "She left in a hurry and left quite a bit of stuff behind."

Of course Lillian had left in a hurry. She had been eluding authorities. She'd had no intention of showing up for that court date. He was surprised that Seymour had been so surprised. She was a Davies. And Jake had warned him.

The landlady shuffled back with a cardboard box

in her hands. She peeled back one of the tabs and peered inside. "Yes, this is Lilly's stuff." She reached inside and said, "Aha, that's why you look so familiar. I found these pictures of you in her place."

Jake took the strip of photos she held out to him. He had a strip of nearly identical photos at home. He and Lillian had taken them in one of those silly photo booths on the pier near the Lake Michigan shoreline. She was smiling up at him in every photo but the last—in that one they were kissing.

His stomach muscles clenched as he remembered leaning down and brushing his lips across hers. She'd tasted so damn sweet, like the cotton candy he'd bought her.

"Those were actually in her trash can," the woman remarked, then shrugged.

Of course the old hoarder had gone through Lillian's trash. But it was fortunate for Jake that she had. He noticed some other letters inside the box and, put together with that strip of photos, he realized exactly where she was hiding.

"I don't understand why she threw them out," the woman remarked. "You are a good-looking son of a gun. Tall, dark and handsome…" She offered him a nearly toothless smile.

He forced himself to smile back. Lillian had rented the upstairs apartment from the older woman who owned the old Victorian house near downtown River City, Michigan. Mrs. Truman—that was her name.

"You haven't been around for a while, but I haven't forgotten about you," the elderly widow teased. "I'm sure Lillian hasn't, either."

Jake wondered if she'd thought of him as much

as he had her. Of course, she hadn't been happy that he'd brought her dad and brother into custody. Her plan must have been to make him fall in love with her so that he wouldn't do his job. That must have been why she'd acted so sweet and innocent when she was really anything but.

She was a thief—just like the rest of her family. And she'd nearly stolen his heart all those months ago. He'd thought he was falling for her, but he hadn't known who she was, either.

"Now, those other men…" The older woman shuddered. "I don't remember them. They claimed to be her friends." She shook her head, and the blond wig she wore slipped slightly, revealing the thin wisps of white hair beneath it. "But you were the only guy I ever saw come around, except for her brothers and her dad."

Her brow furrowed. "But now that I think about it, I haven't seen her family around for a while, either— even before Lilly gave up the apartment."

That was because most of them were behind bars. But he didn't share that information with the elderly woman. He was stuck instead on what else she'd shared with him.

Had Jake been the only boyfriend she'd brought home? As passionate as Lillian had been, he doubted it. The old woman was obviously going senile.

But what if she wasn't?

"What other men?" he asked.

Damn Tuttle. The old bail bondsman wasn't just playing Jake; he was probably also playing him off against the O'Hanigans. Those bounty hunters were ruthless when it came to tracking down a fugitive.

They would go much further than Jake would in order to collect their bounty. Jake looked more closely at the older woman, making certain they hadn't roughed her up any.

She chuckled. "Nobody for you to be jealous of, honey. They had nothing on you."

"Did you show them any of this stuff?" he asked.

She shook her head. "Heavens no, like I said—I didn't recognize them. I don't think they were friends of hers at all, not like you."

He had never been Lillian's friend, either. For a little while, he'd hoped he could be more. But when he'd done his job and apprehended her dad and brother, she'd sworn she would never forgive him.

What would she do when he apprehended her? Because now he knew exactly where she was…

He knew where she was. The thought both thrilled and terrified Lillian. Even as much as she hated him, she had missed him. She'd missed seeing his handsome face with the faint stubble that always shadowed his strong jaw no matter how recently he'd shaved. She'd missed seeing his brown eyes go black with desire when they'd made love.

But that hadn't been love.

That had been deception.

He'd deceived her. That was why she'd been furious with him—not because he'd apprehended her dad and brother but because he'd used her to do it. She didn't approve of the things her family did, and she never would have helped or harbored any of them once they became fugitives. But when other family members had told her dad and brother Dave that she was getting serious about a man, their protective instincts had kicked in and they'd wanted to check him out—to make sure he was good enough for her.

He wasn't, because he was a liar and a sneak. All he'd been after was the bounty for her family. The minute he'd seen them, he'd taken them into custody. And Lillian had told Jake, among several other things, that she never wanted to see him again.

She certainly didn't want to see him now.

She knew he wasn't looking for her to declare his undying love. Or he would have done that months ago. He would have continued to apologize and beg her forgiveness if he'd wanted to see her again. So obviously, he had never cared about her; he'd only been using her. The only reason he wanted to find her now was to bring her in and collect the bounty on her. And doing that would probably get her killed.

"Thanks for calling me, Mrs. Truman," she told her former landlady.

The older woman's voice crackled in the cell phone Lillian had pressed to her ear as she leaned back in the driver's seat. "I'm sorry I showed him what you left behind, honey, but when I dug those photos out of your trash can, I knew that man was special."

If he had truly been special, she wouldn't have thrown the photos away. But she didn't bother pointing that out to Mrs. Truman. However, Lillian had taken those photos out of the trash several times herself. Every time she'd tossed them, something had compelled her to fish them back out. Maybe she'd been holding out hope that he would come back and beg her forgiveness. She hadn't been able to completely give up on him or to completely forget about him.

She touched her belly.

And now she never would. Would the baby look like Jake, with those big dark eyes, chiseled features and naturally tanned-looking skin?

The older woman cackled. "He sure got jealous when I told him about the other men looking for you."

Lillian's heart stopped beating for a moment before resuming at a frantic pace. "Other men?"

"They said they knew you." She paused to inject a derisive snort. "But I never saw them around before."

And Mrs. Truman, despite her age and cataracts, didn't miss a thing.

So how many people were looking for Lillian? Were these guys Tom Kuipers's men or more bounty hunters? Or police officers?

But police officers would have identified themselves. No. It had to be someone else. Someone she wouldn't want to find her any more than she wanted Jake to find her.

"Thanks for letting me know," she said. And she was glad that she'd given the older woman her new cell number. Mrs. Truman didn't have any family to call if something happened to her. She and her late husband had never had children, and their extended families had already passed on, too.

Lillian didn't need to worry about Mrs. Truman right now, though. She wasn't the one that something was about to happen to. It was Lillian. Had she left anything behind that might have given a clue to her whereabouts? She tried to remember what she'd left and what she'd thrown out.

Since Mrs. Truman had fished out the photos, she might have taken the old letters from the trash can, too. Lillian looked through the windshield at the small cottage her maternal grandmother owned.

Gran was in a nursing home now. That was why she hadn't gotten down to her place in Florida. But she was just in the rehabilitation part of the nursing home to recuperate from a broken hip. It was taking a little longer than expected, or maybe not since she was eighty-nine, but with as sharp and feisty as she was, she might be able to live on her own again someday.

Or with Lillian, if Lillian wasn't in prison.

What had happened to the flash drive?

She had to find that evidence—if it hadn't already been destroyed.

A chill raced over her skin with the thought. What if it had been destroyed? She would never be able to get into the office again, never be able to gain access to the records to prove her innocence.

She shivered. She'd shut off the ignition a while ago, since the car had been making odd clunky noises when Mrs. Truman had called. She'd wanted to be able to hear her, so she'd shut off the car and coasted to a stop on the road just a few yards away from the cottage. With the heater off, it had grown cool inside the vintage Buick.

Fortunately, it wasn't her car, so Jake wouldn't recognize it. Knowing that once she failed to appear in court a warrant would be issued for her arrest, she had left her vehicle at the courthouse. Then she'd had a taxi driver bring her to the lakeshore. From there, she had walked to her grandmother's cottage. This was Gran's car, her pride and joy. Like her cottage, she hoped to use it again someday.

"It's good to hear your voice," Mrs. Truman said.

Lillian felt a twinge in her heart. The older woman obviously missed her. She missed her, too. She wanted her life back—the one she'd had before the embezzlement charges. The one she'd had before Jake.

Her baby kicked, as if in protest. And Lillian ran her hand over her belly again. She was happy she was pregnant. She wanted this baby. So she didn't regret making love with Jake. She just wished it had been love and not deception.

"It's been good to hear your voice, too," she told Mrs. Truman. Before her landlady hung up, Lillian thought to ask, "How long ago was he there?"

"Who? Tall, dark and handsome?"

Despite her resentment of Jake, Lillian smiled. "Yes."

The older lady paused as if looking around for a clock. Or her TV. She judged time by her shows as much as the hands on a clock. "He was here during *Wheel*," she replied, "so over an hour ago."

Which was more than enough time for him to have made it to the cottage. Lillian glanced down the street at the little yellow structure, but she saw no other vehicles parked near it. And the inside of the cabin was as dark as it was outside. It looked as empty as it had when Lillian had arrived earlier that day.

Nobody was there.

Was *he*?

She felt a flutter in her belly and pressed her hand over it. Was it the baby? Or nerves?

Usually the baby kicked hard, and she had no doubt it was him or her moving around inside her—as if the baby felt trapped and was anxious to get out. He or she still had a few weeks to go, though.

No. Lillian felt sick now with nerves.

She couldn't stay here now. Did she have enough time to go inside and grab the bag she hadn't even bothered to unpack? The car wasn't the only thing Gran had had to leave at the cottage. She had a gun, too. And even with her concealed weapons permit, it hadn't been allowed in the nursing home.

Years ago, she'd taught Lillian how to shoot the gun. Maybe she should grab that, too. Lillian didn't care who was coming after her.

She was *not* going to jail.

"Who the hell is he?" Tom Kuipers demanded to know. He divided his attention between the cell phone in his hand and the doors to his den. Beyond those French doors, he had a house full of people.

None of them could overhear this conversation.

None of the who's who of River City society could know what he had done, what he really was. Not a one of them was smart enough to suspect the truth, not even his wife and father-in-law who owned the building equipment and supply company from which Tom had taken all that money. He had fooled them all—just like he'd fooled Lillian Davies.

"I don't know," the man replied. "I didn't see him flash a badge at the old woman or anything."

Would the police be looking for Lillian Davies already, though? She'd just missed the first court date. And it wasn't as if she was being tried for murder.

Maybe he should have framed her for that, too. He had a few people he'd like to kill, but the first was Lillian Davies herself.

"So whoever the hell showed up at her old place—he's not a lawman?" Tom asked.

A long silence was his reply.

"Well?"

"I don't know," the man finally answered him. "He carried himself a certain way, like ex-military or former Secret Service or something."

Tom heard a voice from someone else talking inside the vehicle they were driving as they tailed the guy they'd seen at Lillian Davies's apartment. But that other man speaking wasn't close enough to the cell phone to be understood.

"What?" he asked impatiently.

He hated this, hated not knowing what the hell was going on. And most of all, he hated not knowing where the hell she was and if she had that damn flash drive with her.

Maybe she was more like her notorious family than the naive young girl he'd thought she was.

"He was armed," the man replied. "Wilson saw a holster under his coat."

Who the hell was this guy? Some Rambo wannabe?

Tom cursed. Who else was looking for Lillian Davies and why? Maybe the authorities were already involved and looking for her. After all, when she hadn't shown up in court, she had jumped bail.

So maybe this guy was a bounty hunter.

"We don't have time for this," he said. Especially now. Voices rose behind the door as his guests milled around the estate that also belonged to his wife and father-in-law. Tom was pretty much just a damn guest, too. But he'd started to turn that around when he'd taken all that money.

Pretty soon he would have more than they had. And he would no longer need either of them.

Laughter rang out. People were close. His wife was probably showing guests around the house. She wouldn't hesitate to barge into his den, even though it was the one part of the house that was supposed to be his alone.

He lowered his voice and spoke quickly but succinctly into the phone. "Lillian Davies needs to be found and eliminated. *Now.*"

Before she could turn over that flash drive—if it actually existed—to the authorities.

"What about the big guy?" his man asked, and there was a faint crackle of nerves in his voice. Or maybe it had just been the phone.

There were seven or eight of them. They couldn't be afraid of one man. And if they were, Tom needed to hire tougher guys. At least these weren't the only men he had working on this special assignment.

"If he gets in the way," Tom said, "eliminate him, too." He didn't care who the hell he was. Tom had come too far to go back now. He was too close to pulling off the plan.

Chapter 3

Jake was so close. He dragged in a deep breath and could smell her scent yet inside the cottage. It was like flowers and grass after a summer rain—fresh and new. She had been here recently, maybe just moments ago.

How the hell had he missed her?

He'd parked down the block at the empty lot for the beach access. But it was after dark, so nobody else had been there. Nobody was here, either.

After seeing those old letters from her grandmother, he'd realized this was where she'd be. And he'd found the little yellow cottage easily because he'd been here before, that day they'd taken those photos in the booth on the beach. He'd been pressing her to introduce him to her family. So she'd brought him to meet her elderly grandmother.

It hadn't been what he'd had in mind, but he'd certainly enjoyed meeting her grandmother more than he had any of the rest of her family. Gran wasn't a Davies and had had less use for the family her now-deceased daughter had married into than even Jake had. While she loved her grandsons, too, the only one she trusted and respected was her granddaughter.

Where was Gran?

He couldn't believe the octogenarian would have willingly left her house. Maybe finding out that her precious granddaughter was no different than the other Davies had killed her, because the old woman had told him the only way she'd leave this place was in a pine box.

And he hadn't blamed her. The cottage had access to and a breathtaking view of Lake Michigan with its gorgeous sunsets.

Was that where Lillian had gone? Down to the beach? He started toward the door when he heard the knob rattle. He'd turned on no lights so he wouldn't alert her to his presence. He had also locked the door behind him for the same reason.

Of course, he'd remembered where the hide-a-key was kept, too—in the little birdhouse, which was an exact replica of the yellow cottage her grandfather had made for her grandmother. Lillian had wistfully remarked how she envied their love and wanted one like that for herself someday. Then she'd looked at him—with those ocean-blue eyes of hers—and something had shifted inside his chest.

It must have been fear—because he felt it now when the door blasted open and gunfire erupted. He ducked and drew his weapon.

What the hell?

Where had they come from? There was more than one shooter. Glass shattered as the windows were shot out. Wood chipped off the bead-board cabinets and the shabby-chic furniture. Jake raised his weapon and returned fire.

Unless they'd gotten a hell of a lot more zealous than they'd been before, these were not the O'Hanigans. Even they wouldn't have gone to these extremes to bring back a jumper for a bounty.

Lillian wasn't wanted dead or alive, at least not by the law. So who the hell else was after her? And why were they so willing to take him out along with her?

The gunfire erupted, shattering the silence of the summer night. Lillian could see the flashes of the shots inside the dark cabin. She could also see glass exploding from the windows and bullets ripping through the walls. She gasped in shock and horror.

Gran's little haven was being destroyed. Because of Lillian…

They had to be after her. Had they gone inside and just started shooting up the place?

Were they that determined to kill her?

Lillian needed to get the hell out of there. Her hands shaking, she reached for the keys dangling from the ignition. She turned them but the ignition just clicked. The engine didn't turn over; it didn't even rumble. And she remembered that it had sounded funny before she'd heard her cell ringing. She'd shut it off and coasted to a stop on the road just a few yards from the cottage.

The gas gauge proclaimed it had half of a tank.

But it had been stuck there since she'd started using it, and she'd driven it all the way into the city to her lawyer's office building. Oh, no, the gauge was probably broken. She had no gas. No way of escaping.

While she'd been working up the nerve to go inside the cottage and retrieve Gran's gun and her clothes, she'd seen a van pull in to the short driveway. At least half a dozen men, maybe more, had jumped out and headed for the cottage. She should have run then.

She needed to run now. She threw open the door and headed toward the lot down at the beach. Someone might have left a vehicle there. Sometimes people walked the beach at night, despite it being closed after dark. Tools clanged inside her big purse. She didn't have the gun. But she had other weapons she could use.

She blew out a breath of relief when she found an older truck parked in the lot. Hopefully, it didn't have an alarm system. She pulled a slim jim from her bag and, slipping it between the window and the door, unlocked the door. Then she pulled it open and reached under the dash for the wires.

She hadn't been old enough to drive when her oldest brother, Dave, had taught her how to hot-wire a car. He'd insisted she would need to know how someday. She hadn't—until today. Could she remember what he'd shown her?

She reached into her bag for the flashlight she'd also stashed in there. She needed to know what color the wires were to remember which ones to splice together. But before she could turn on the flashlight, she heard someone coming—footsteps pounding across the asphalt as they ran—straight toward her.

Had he seen her get out of the Buick and run down here? Was he chasing her? Since she hadn't heard those footsteps until now, she didn't think he'd seen her yet.

So she jumped into the truck and pulled the door shut. Maybe she could hide in there. But before she could lock it, he pulled open the door and jumped in beside her, his broad shoulder and hip bumping against her side with such force that he slid her across the long bench seat. She turned away to protect her belly.

"What the hell?" he exclaimed between pants for breath. Then he must have recognized her because he exclaimed, "Lillian!"

Her heart slammed against her ribs with shock at Jake's sudden appearance. He had definitely found her. Or maybe she had inadvertently found him.

"Were you stealing my truck?" he asked, as he noticed the wires dangling below the dash.

Before she could reply, the back window shattered with another blast of gunfire. He pushed her off the seat and onto the floor as he jammed a key in the ignition and started the engine. Tires squealing and gravel flying, he steered the pickup out of the parking lot.

"Friends of yours?" he asked. "Or family?"

"I don't know who they are," she replied. But she had a very good idea who had sent them. Tom Kuipers.

"Did they hit you?" she asked with concern. He must have been inside that cottage with them—with all those bullets flying.

"No," he said, "which probably disappoints you to no end."

She'd once considered shooting him herself not that long ago. But she couldn't imagine actually hurting him or wanting him hurt. There had already been enough pain between them. Unfortunately, all that pain had been hers when he had shattered her trust and broken her heart.

She flinched as the baby kicked her ribs. Her last ultrasound hadn't been able to determine the sex, but the baby had to be a boy. He was already causing her pain, too, just like his father. Crouched on the floor, she hid her belly behind her raised knees. She didn't want Jake to see that she was pregnant and it was easier to hide in the dark. She had never wanted him to know—unless he came to her of his own accord. Not to take her to jail, but to apologize for what he'd done. She didn't think he'd shown up tonight to apologize. But unless she jumped out of the speeding truck, she didn't know how she was going to get away from him now.

More gunshots rang out, pinging off the metal of the truck. The side mirror broke, sending bits of glass and plastic flying. She gasped in fear.

She didn't have to worry about getting away from Jake right now. She had to worry about staying alive.

"Stay down!" he yelled at her over the sound of the wind rushing through the shattered windows.

Even if she hadn't been paralyzed with fear, she wasn't about to move, not at the risk of getting hit by one of the flying bullets.

"And hang on," he added, as he jerked the wheel and careened around a corner.

Lillian's shoulder bumped against the passenger's door, and she grimaced. But she wasn't worried about her shoulder. She was worried about her baby. She couldn't risk anything happening to her unborn child—to their unborn child.

"You have to slow down!" she yelled back at him.

"If I slow down, they'll catch us," he countered.

But he must have slowed down enough that the van had caught up with them because something rammed against the back bumper, sending the pickup into a spin.

Lillian grabbed tightly on to the seat and screamed. Earlier she'd been worried about losing her freedom. Now she was worried about losing her life.

What the hell had Donny Davies done? Guilt weighed heavily on his thin chest, making it difficult for him to breathe.

Lillian had trusted him...

But then the rest of the family had trusted her. And she'd betrayed them with that damn bounty hunter, Jake Howard. She had literally been sleeping with the enemy. She claimed she hadn't known who he was. But she hadn't stepped in and stopped the man from taking Dad and Dave into custody. From collecting his bounty.

Sure, she'd been crying, but it had been about the man lying to her. Not about her family getting arrested. Just like Gran, she'd always disapproved of the things some of the Davies family did.

She and Gran would certainly disapprove of what Donny had done. But Dad and Dave had declared that they owed her nothing now...

She was no longer one of them.

But since she hadn't shown up for court that day, she was a fugitive now. So maybe for the first time in her twenty-five years, Lillian was one of them.

What would it cost her?

Her freedom?

Or her life?

The people after her were more dangerous than Donny had realized. And he had betrayed them, too. But unlike her, he had a place to hide where no one would find him.

Not even her.

He lay in the dark, unable to sleep, barely breathing, as he fingered the plastic device in his hand. What the hell should he do with it?

The right thing?

The thing his sister had asked him to do in the first place? Just like she'd asked him to stick with school and not resort to the life of crime the rest of their family lived. But Davieses rarely did the right thing.

Even Lillian.

She had made some big mistakes. Jake Howard was the biggest one, though. It was his fault that it had come to this, that her own family had turned against her.

So whatever happened to her was Jake's fault.

Not his…

Chapter 4

His knuckles ached, straining from his efforts, as Jake clutched the steering wheel, fighting to keep it from spinning out of his grasp as the old truck careened wildly across the road.

Crouched yet in the small space between the dash and the front seat, Lillian screamed in fear. It wasn't safe for her down there. She could hit her head on the passenger's door or the dash. But it was better than getting it blown off.

The men in the van kept firing at them. Bullets pinged off the metal and cracked what was left of the glass.

He steered the truck out of the tailspin the van had sent it into when it had slammed into the rear bumper. Before the men could catch up again, Jake pressed hard on the accelerator. The truck jerked forward, and Lillian's forehead bumped against the dash.

"Are you all right?" he asked.

"No!" Her voice cracked with fear.

At least she hadn't lost consciousness.

Unfortunately, he hadn't lost the van yet, either. Bright lights glinted off his rearview mirror as the van accelerated, too, closing the distance between the vehicles again. He had to move faster.

"Hang on!" he warned her. Then he gunned the engine.

A whimper of fear slipped between her lips. He wanted to reach out and reassure her. But then he reminded himself that this was all her fault. Those men were shooting at them because of *her*.

"You must know who these guys are," he insisted. "They showed up at *your* grandma's house."

"They must have followed *you* there," she said.

Damn it. She was right. If these were the guys Mrs. Truman had talked about, the ones who'd shown up at Lillian's place, they hadn't seen the things she'd left behind six months ago. They couldn't have learned what he had. But they might have staked out her apartment in case she showed up there. And they'd seen him instead.

"They probably don't even know I'm in this truck," she continued.

And they might not. He hadn't known that she was inside it when he'd jumped into his truck. But she hadn't just been inside it, she'd been trying to steal it. She couldn't have known the rusted old pickup was his, though.

Could she?

He hadn't used this vehicle when he'd been dating her. He'd used his pleasure vehicle instead, an old Chevrolet Nova he'd restored himself. This old truck was his work vehicle because its big block engine had more power. But at the moment it wasn't fast enough.

"The last place I was before driving out here was your apartment. If they followed me..." And how the hell had they managed that without his noticing? "...then they followed me from there."

The truck lurched forward as the van struck again. Metal crunched. He wasn't sure if it was the truck's rear bumper or the front of the van. He hoped like hell it was the front of the van. Maybe they'd disable their own damn vehicle.

"Lose them!" she yelled at him.

Her voice cracked now with anger. She wasn't the sweet soft-spoken woman he remembered and whom he'd spent the past eight months missing. But then she must have never actually been that woman—the one he had started to fall for.

No, she was definitely a Davies.

Not that she didn't have every right to be mad, with people shooting at them and trying to run them off the road.

Jake's pulse pounded with fury. He couldn't remember the last time he'd been so angry. He could remember the last time he'd felt helpless, though— when Lillian had sobbed heartbrokenly as he'd taken her dad and oldest brother into custody. He hadn't been able to make her understand he'd just been doing his job.

But he suspected now that she'd always known

who he was. She'd probably been playing him just as she must have played her boss when she'd embezzled money from the company for which she'd worked.

No matter what she'd done, though, he didn't want anyone to hurt her. And with the way those guys had opened fire in the cottage, it certainly looked as though someone was trying to kill them. Jake didn't intend to die, and he sure as hell wasn't going to let anyone harm Lillian.

He pressed harder on the accelerator. But then he took one hand from the steering wheel and pulled his gun from his holster. He extended it through the shot-out back window and using the rearview mirror, he took aim and fired at the van. Over and over again.

Glass shattered and the van tires squealed as it braked and then slipped into a skid. While it careened out of control behind them, Jake accelerated more and increased the distance between them. Despite this, he was tempted to turn back and find out who the hell they were and if he'd hit any of them…

But he glanced down at Lillian crouched yet on the floorboards, and he knew that he couldn't risk it. He couldn't risk her life.

If he hadn't been outnumbered…

But even if he'd hit one or two of them, he would still be outnumbered. There had been so many of them firing at him in her grandmother's house.

They had to be after her.

And he intended to find out why.

He steered around a couple of sharp hairpin curves, nearly raising the truck onto two wheels as he did. Then he spied a slight space between trees on the side of the street. It was probably some old two-track road leading back to an old cabin or an oil well. He braked and turned onto the nearly obscured trail. He turned so fast that the truck nearly flipped over on the passenger's side.

And Lillian screamed again.

"Sorry," he said. "I'm trying to lose them." And so far it looked as though he had.

The truck bounced along the rough road, as he continued down the two-track, deeper into the trees. Night had fallen, but the moon was big and bright enough that it might reveal their location unless he drove farther from the main road. Of course, if those guys found them Jake wouldn't be able to escape with the truck.

He and Lillian would have to outrun the men on foot. As shot up as the truck was, that might not be a bad idea, even now. He wasn't sure how much farther the beat-up old pickup could make it.

He stopped the truck and glanced out the back window to make sure they were deep enough into the woods so that they wouldn't be seen from the road. But before he could even put the vehicle in Park, the passenger's door opened—flashing on the dome light as she jumped out.

"Lillian!"

If the van went past and saw the light in the trees, their hiding place was blown. But she seemed more intent on getting away from him than the shooters.

Had she set up the ambush?

Jake followed her out and slammed the door shut behind him. But he couldn't see her in the trees. He could only hear the occasional snap of a branch and the rustle of brush as she ran. She wasn't getting away from him that easily.

But as he started after her, he heard the squeal of tires against pavement as a vehicle braked on the street. Maybe finding her was the least of his concerns right now. He had to worry instead that they had been found. And if the shooters had been determined to kill him before, they would be even more determined now that he had fired back at them.

Who the hell was after Lillian?

And where the hell had she gone?

Branches slapped Lillian in the face, making her gasp in shock and pain as she rushed through the underbrush. Twigs snapped beneath her feet and briars caught her pants, tugging on the thin knit maternity leggings. She heard fabric tear and felt the sting of the thorns scratching her skin.

Tears stung her eyes at the pain. But she rushed ahead, even though she had no idea where she was going. She didn't even have any idea where she *was*. She might keep running and fall right off a bluff into Lake Michigan.

This wasn't smart. But neither was staying where men were shooting and trying to run her off the road. Had they been looking for her at all? She hadn't been in the cottage. And they couldn't have known that she had been in the truck with Jake. Nobody had been around when she'd jumped into it.

So who were they really after?

Since they had shown up at her grandmother's cottage, she suspected it was her—just as Jake had claimed—and he had just gotten caught in the cross fire. But she couldn't trust him to protect her. He'd already proved that she couldn't trust him at all.

Briars and brush tripped her, and she stumbled forward, falling onto her knees. A curse slipped through her lips as she reached for her belly, pressing her hands over it. She hadn't fallen on the mound that was her baby, though. And she hadn't hit the baby bump on the dash or the door while the men had been crashing into the truck and Jake had been driving like a mad man.

He was mad now.

She'd heard him shout her name just as she'd slipped into the trees and the darkness. She needed to get up and keep running. But her lungs burned and she struggled to breathe.

It wasn't just the exertion from her run that had stolen her breath away. It was fear.

Men had been shooting at them.

Trying to run them off the road.

She'd suspected before how much danger she'd been in. That was why she'd spent the past six months awaiting her court date hiding out in Florida. But now she knew for certain. Somebody had literally come gunning for her. And it hadn't been just Jake.

Jake…

The baby leaped beneath her palms. He was doing somersaults, just like Lillian's heart was within her chest. Every snap of a twig or branch made it flip again. Somebody was coming after her.

And it didn't matter if it was one of those armed gunmen or Jake, she had to run. She had to get away. She couldn't let anyone catch her.

She couldn't let anyone catch them.

She rubbed her palms over her belly again before she moved her hands to the ground and pushed herself to her feet. It wasn't easy to move quickly—not now. Just getting up from a chair took a concerted effort because of the size of her belly. And it—and her baby—was still growing.

She had weeks yet to go. She couldn't go into early labor, couldn't risk her baby coming too soon. Or worse yet, not coming at all.

She needed to be careful. But staying behind to get shot or dragged back to jail was more dangerous than running through the woods in the dark.

Wasn't it?

She wasn't sure what was in the woods, either. Gran had told her that dangerous animals had recently been spotted in the area. Coyotes. Black bears.

She was less worried about the four-legged animals than she was the two, so she forced herself to keep going through the woods. Maybe she would come upon another road and a car she could wave down to drive her away. But did anyone stop for hitchhikers anymore?

She wasn't just any hitchhiker, though. She was an obviously pregnant one. Surely, someone would take pity on her and offer to help her.

First, she had to find that road, though. The woods just kept getting thicker and thicker, the trees growing taller and closer together, the underbrush so dense she could barely fight her way through it. As she crashed into an impenetrable wall of briar bushes, her breath escaped in a hiss of pain.

But before she could turn back to find a way around that thorny wall, a strong hand wrapped tightly around her arm. She couldn't see who had grabbed her. She could see nothing but darkness and the faint shadows of the tall trees.

She parted her lips to scream, but before any sound could escape, a palm clasped over her mouth—muffling her voice and her breath.

Was this person trying to silence her for just the moment or forever? If it was one of the thugs that Mr. Kuipers must have sent after her, it was undoubtedly meant to silence her forever.

Seymour Tuttle jumped as the phone on his desk rang. He should have been expecting it. As a bondsman, his phone rang constantly with people needing to be bailed out. Generally, they needed to wait until morning before a judge set the bail amount. But often Seymour was the first call they made from jail—so he'd be ready to post their bond when they were able to get out.

If they were able to get out…

Why had the judge granted Lillian Davies bail? Based on her family history alone, she should have been ruled a flight risk. But why had Seymour posted that bail, especially after Jake had warned him against ever bonding out another Davies?

No matter how old he was, and he didn't want to think about how old that was, he was still a sucker for a pretty face. And they didn't come much prettier than Lillian Davies. Although she looked like an angel with her pale blond hair and blue eyes, she was apparently a devil like the rest of her damn family. At least that was what Jake Howard believed.

Maybe this was Jake calling him with an update. The guy was good—his best damn bounty hunter.

With a sigh, he dropped his greasy burger onto his desk, wiped his hand on the polyester pants which matched the polyester suit jacket slung over the back of his chair and picked up the phone. "Tuttle Bonds…"

"Tuttle," a raspy voice said.

It wasn't Jake's. His was even deeper than this guy's, if it was even a guy calling and not someone just disguising her voice. Sometimes people did that from jail because they were embarrassed at having been arrested. And like Seymour was going to record their call and broadcast it.

He didn't care about his clients' reputations. He only cared about getting his money.

"Yeah, this is Tuttle," he confirmed for the caller.

"Did you send someone after Lillian Davies?"

Speak of the devil…

Or speaking to her?

No. Her voice had been too light and soft ever to become this raspy.

"That's none of your business," he remarked.

"It's a matter of public record that you posted her bail," the voice replied. Irritation cleared away some of the fake raspiness. The caller was a man, but Seymour wasn't sure if he'd ever heard the voice before.

Could it be one of her brothers? Or her dad? Of course, then the call would have come from prison and he would have needed to accept the charges. No. It couldn't be one of them—at least not one of the ones Jake had already apprehended for Seymour and the courts.

"That's public record," Seymour agreed. "Not whether or not I sent someone after her."

"Stands to reason you'll want your money back."

"Stands to reason," Seymour agreed.

"But if you're a reasonable man, you'll forget about the money."

"I will?" Now he was intrigued. Just what the hell was this caller's agenda? To have him let Lillian Davies go?

"Yeah, I'm sure you value your life much more than you do your wallet." The line clicked and went dead before Seymour could laugh.

Whoever had called didn't know him very damn well. Of course he valued his wallet over his life. Without money, life wasn't worth living anyway.

If this caller had meant to scare him off, he'd done just the opposite. He'd only made Seymour that much more determined to bring her in.

Had it been a member of her family who'd called him? But most of them knew him. They knew that he wouldn't back down from tracing a skip. So if it wasn't a Davies, who the hell else was involved with Lillian Davies and why didn't he want her brought to jail?

Seymour needed to get hold of Jake and find out what the guy had learned so far. Of course, he hadn't been on the case very long. But then Jake had never needed much time—except that last time—to track down a Davies.

He'd taken weeks to bring in Lillian's dad and brother Dave. And Seymour couldn't help but wonder if during those weeks, something had happened between Jake and Lillian—something that Jake hadn't wanted to talk about.

Not that Jake ever wanted to talk.

All he wanted to do was his job. And that was why he was Seymour's best bounty hunter. Had the hunter caught his bounty yet?

He punched in the speed dial for Jake's cell, but the phone rang several times before finally going to voice mail. And a strange chill chased down Seymour's spine.

How the hell had that caller known he'd sent someone after Lillian? Had he run into Jake?

Had something happened to Seymour's best bounty hunter?

Chapter 5

*D*amn it!

Jake had pressed his hand over Lillian's mouth to keep her quiet, but then his phone kept vibrating in his pocket. While the ringer was off, the vibration let off a sound—one that seemed loud in the silence of the woods.

Lillian struggled in his grasp, trying to break free of him. Then she clawed at his arms, so that he loosened his grip on her and his palm slipped away from her mouth. Partially free of his grasp, she jerked forward only to cringe and whimper as she struck that wall of briar bushes again.

The woods were full of briars and thorn bushes, and she must have lost a few strands of hair on each one. That was how he'd tracked her: every pale blond strand had glistened in the moonlight as if they were strands of light instead of strands of hair.

"Careful," he whispered. "You're going to hurt yourself." If she hadn't already…

He knew from experience how soft and silky her skin was. She probably had several scratches and scrapes. He felt a few on his arms, and his skin was hardly soft and silky. Of course, those scratches were from her nails.

He remembered how they'd felt running down his back as he'd moved inside her and she'd writhed beneath him, seeking release. Despite her sweetness, she'd been so passionate. But he knew now, she wasn't really that sweet.

"Jake," she gasped his name.

"Shh," he said, as he peered into the darkness. He couldn't see much more than shadows, but he knew those men were out there. The sharp snap of twigs breaking echoed throughout the forest. "They'll find us."

They must have seen that moment when the dome light had flashed on—because the van had stopped on the road. And unfortunately, he must not have hit any of them when he'd fired at them. Or they would have been heading to a hospital instead of crashing through the woods, searching for them.

Damn it!

Who the hell were these guys? They were nearly as determined as he was to catch Lillian. Or was it really her they were after? Had they seen her in the truck with him before he'd shoved her below the dash?

He'd made some enemies as a bounty hunter and

even more before that, as a US marshal. But nobody had recently come after him. The only person who'd been bothering Jake was Lillian. But that was just in his dreams, when he'd managed to sleep at all the past eight months.

So Jake couldn't know for certain who these guys were really after—unless they caught them. And he wasn't going to allow that to happen.

"Come on," he whispered, and he grasped her arm again. This time he led her through the woods. But as he led her, his phone began to vibrate again.

"Shh," she murmured to him.

A curse slipped through his lips. Whoever the hell was calling him needed to give up. He didn't have time to talk at the moment. And if he did, it was Lillian he'd talk to; he wanted to know what the hell was going on, why these men were after her, if she was the intended target.

Had Seymour subcontracted with more bounty hunters than him and the O'Hanigans? As if the O'Hanigans weren't bad enough.

Jake was tempted to pitch his phone into the underbrush. But he might need it to call for backup. Not that he had many options. Since leaving the US Marshals, he worked alone, although he had a few old contacts he could call if he got in a jam.

But he'd never gotten into anything he hadn't been able to get out of, except Lillian. Something had happened when he'd been seeing her; he'd felt like he was going under and that he'd never break free to the surface again.

But that was before he'd learned about her arrest and had finally been able to see her clearly. Figuratively, at least. Literally, he could barely see her now. She was just a shadow beside him, except for her silvery blond hair. That would be like a beacon drawing the gunmen toward them. He needed to find a place to hide her.

The pungent odor of pines reached his nose. And for the first time in a long time, he let in a memory from his childhood—one of hiding beneath the pines in his backyard. It was what he'd been hiding from that he blocked from rushing back. He had to stay focused right now.

He crouched low and tugged Lillian down beside him. She moved slowly, though—almost too slowly. Once she was on the ground next to him, he pulled back the low boughs of the nearest pine tree and, leaning close, whispered in her ear, "Crawl under there."

She shivered. It was colder here—in the darkness of the woods—and damp near the ground. She might have hesitated just because she was cold, but when another twig snapped nearby, she froze entirely.

Jake reached out to push her under the bough and as he touched her waist, he felt a jolt. It wasn't tiny like he remembered. It was swollen over her distended belly. As he slid his hand over that belly, he felt another jolt as a little foot kicked him.

She was pregnant.

He'd had questions for her before, but now he had only one: *Is it mine?*

But he couldn't ask that. He couldn't ask anything because the brush was rustling, twigs snapping, and he knew the men were closing in on them. He had to lead them away from Lillian, especially now that he knew there was no way she could outrun those men.

"Stay here," he whispered. "I'll come back when it's safe."

If he survived…

But he had to survive now. If he didn't, there was no way she'd escape those men on her own.

Safe for whom?

It wasn't safe for Lillian, not now that Jake had felt her belly. He knew she was pregnant. Did he realize the baby was his?

Maybe not.

She hoped not.

Not that she expected him to take any responsibility for their baby. He hadn't taken any responsibility when he'd used her to apprehend her dad and oldest brother.

He hadn't cared then that he'd broken her heart. He'd only cared about collecting his bounty for apprehending the fugitives.

How high was the price on her head now?

Maybe those other men weren't Tom Kuipers's minions. Maybe they were bounty hunters like Jake, and like Jake, they were ruthless enough to use whatever means necessary to apprehend her.

At least he'd only taken her heart. The way these guys had fired into the cottage and then tried to run them off the road, they seemed determined to take her life.

"Over here!" someone shouted.

"You've got the woman?" another called out.

And she tensed, worried that her hiding place had been discovered.

"I don't see her," the first voice replied, "but I saw the man run that way. She's probably with him."

She heard the snap and crack of twigs and branches as the men chased after Jake. He'd led them away from her. And away from where the vehicles had been left.

He'd told her to stay put and wait for his return. But there were a lot of men after him. There was no guarantee that he would return.

Pain clenched her heart at the thought of him getting hurt. Or worse…

How could she still care so much after the way he'd treated her? After the way he'd acted since seeing her again? He seemed angry with her, like he was somehow the victim when she was the one he'd used.

And the one that Tom Kuipers had framed.

But Jake hadn't given her a chance to explain that she wasn't guilty of those charges—not that they'd had a chance to talk yet. Maybe she shouldn't have thrown open the passenger's door and ran. But her instincts had been screaming at her to escape, not just the men but Jake, as well.

Maybe Jake more than the men. She hadn't wanted him to see that she was pregnant. She hadn't wanted him to know that he was going to be a father. She hadn't believed that a man as heartless as he had proven to be could be a loving father to a child.

Her baby kicked again, and she knew why she cared about Jake despite how much he'd hurt her. Because even though she had every reason to hate him, she loved the baby Jake had given her. She hadn't planned for him or her. But Lillian was very happy that she was pregnant.

And she wanted her baby to be safe and secure. Lillian needed to get her and her unborn child the hell out of there. Holding her breath, she listened and waited until the rustling of brush faded far into the distance.

Then she crawled from beneath those low-lying pine boughs and pushed herself up from the ground to her feet again. She moved more quietly now, following the path beaten down through the brush back to where the truck was parked. She'd thought she had been running for so long, but she hadn't gone that great a distance from the vehicle. It was as if she'd been running in quicksand.

She moved faster now as she approached the truck. Running around the front, she reached for the driver's door. But before she opened it, she remembered the dome light flashing on and alerting the men in the van to where they had stopped. She shouldn't have done that.

But she had been almost as anxious to escape Jake as she was those men, maybe even more so now. She peered through the driver's window and saw no keys dangling from the ignition. Her hands were shaking too badly right now for her to try to hot-wire the truck, if she could even remember how Dave had showed her to do it.

She glanced toward the road. The white van was visible through the trees, parked on the shoulder where the two-track road began.

Had the men blocked their escape?

She probably wouldn't be able to drive around that van even if she was able to start the truck before the men returned. Were they all chasing Jake through the woods? Was the van sitting empty?

Realizing it might be her best option to escape, she crouched low and used the brush for cover as she moved toward the road and the van. The front window, which had shattered like a spiderweb, lay crumpled on the hood, as if someone had shoved it out so they could see through it. But she saw no one sitting behind the steering wheel. Since the van was on the road and clear of the trees, the moon shone inside it, illuminating the front.

Lillian could see no one inside. They must all be chasing after Jake. She felt a twinge in her heart again—a twinge of fear for him. She wanted him to be safe, too.

But Jake could take care of himself. He wouldn't have survived his years as a US marshal and as a bad-ass bounty hunter if he weren't tough. Lillian didn't need to worry about him.

She needed to worry about their baby. It was her responsibility to take care of him or her. She smoothed her palm over her belly where the baby kicked again. He or she must have been feeling all the fear and anxiety that coursed through Lillian.

She had to get the hell out of there—away from those men and Jake. So she moved around the front of the van and reached for the driver's door. As she opened it, that damn dome light flashed on, so she jumped quickly inside and swung the door closed behind her and extinguished the light.

The glow of the moon was illumination enough to see the keys that dangled from the ignition. She didn't even have to try to hot-wire it. But as she reached for the keys to turn them and start the van, she heard something…

A cock of a gun, and she felt the barrel press against her temple. This wasn't Jake. There was no way he could have circled back around without her knowing it. And even if he had, she doubted he would have pressed a gun to her head.

He couldn't be that angry with her. Nor could he ever be that ruthless, especially after he'd discovered she was pregnant. No. This had to be one of the gunmen. They weren't all chasing after Jake. One of them had her.

"This damn well better be good news," Tom growled into the phone as he picked it up. It was late now—so late that all the who's who of River City were gone, the party long over and he had already fallen asleep until the ringing cell had awakened him.

Fortunately, the ringing had not woken up his wife. She lay on her back, snoring away. He would have killed that bitch if he'd thought he could get away with it. But he knew he'd be blamed if anything happened to her.

So he'd found another way to get rid of her. Take all of her and her rich daddy's money.

A smile curved his lips as he thought of his escape. Everything was in place. Well, almost in place.

He slid out of bed and walked into the bathroom. After closing the door between it and the master bedroom, he asked, "Did you kill her?"

"Not yet…"

"Not yet!" Rage coursed through him, chasing away the last vestiges of sleep. Hell, he would probably be awake the rest of the night now. "It shouldn't be this damn hard to catch that stupid little girl!"

But she'd already been missing for months.

He should have tried harder to find her then. But he'd been certain that she'd show up for court, and she'd be convicted and sentenced to jail. He didn't really believe that flash drive existed.

Despite the flicker of doubt he felt now and then.

"I've...got...her." The man finally spoke again, but he sounded winded, like it was a struggle for him to talk at all.

Tom didn't know which one it was. He didn't think he'd talked directly to this guy before. But usually his men didn't talk, they just listened.

And followed orders.

"Then why isn't she dead?" Tom impatiently asked him.

"Uh..." The guy's voice trailed off again. He sounded weak.

Tom hated weakness. "Why not?" he demanded to know.

Had she said something about the flash drive? Had she threatened that it would be turned over to the authorities if something happened to her?

"She's pregnant."

Thinking of all the times his wife had begged him over the years to start a family, Tom snorted. What was the big deal about getting pregnant and having babies?

"What the hell does that have to do with anything?" he asked.

The guy had been fine with killing a woman. Why get squeamish about killing a pregnant one?

"I—I—uh…" the man stammered.

His patience gone, Tom sighed. "Bring her to me," he said. "I want to talk to her first anyway." He wanted to find out what the hell had happened to that flash drive—if it even existed in the first place.

"To—to the house?" the man asked.

What an idiot!

"Hell, no!" he growled. If any woman was going to die within these walls, it was going to be his wife.

Maybe he would find a way to do that anyhow, a way where he would not be blamed.

"Bring her to the warehouse," he ordered. He didn't wait for the man to agree. He knew that he would, so he just disconnected the call.

It was better this way. Tom would get his answers from little Miss Lillian Davies. And once he knew the truth about that damn flash drive, then he would pull the trigger and kill her himself.

Yeah, this was better.

When he killed her himself, he would send a message to his men to never mess with him and he would have the assurance that she was no longer a problem.

Chapter 6

Lillian's lungs burned with the breath she'd been holding since that barrel had pressed against her temple. Even though the man had pulled the gun away to take out his cell phone and make a call, she hadn't released it.

She'd overheard that call. The cell phone must have been on speaker because she had listened to every vicious word her former boss had spoken. She had no doubt now that the man, even after learning she was pregnant, wanted her dead. As if framing her for a crime hadn't been cruel enough...

Tears stung her eyes, but she blinked them back. She wasn't giving up yet. She still had time to escape, especially when she heard her captor place another call.

"Not now, Jimmy." The voice emanated from the speaker of the man's cell phone.

Jimmy must have been the man left behind in the van. Why hadn't she noticed him right away?

"We'll get you to the hospital," the man assured him, "once we find her."

Jimmy was hurt. That was why he'd stayed in the van, why he must have been lying in the back when she'd looked through that open front window. How badly was he hurt?

Bad enough that she could overpower him?

"I've got her," Jimmy interrupted. "She walked right up to the van and climbed inside with me."

"Did you do it yet?" the guy asked, his voice rising with excitement. "Did you kill her?"

"The boss wants us to bring her to the warehouse," Jimmy replied with obvious relief. "He wants to be the one to pull the trigger. Get back here. You need to drive."

Jimmy must have been too injured to drive. So he would probably be too injured to chase her if she could manage to escape.

She reached for the door handle. And that barrel pressed against her temple again.

"Don't even try it," Jimmy warned her. Then he told the man on the phone, "Hurry the hell up!"

He was worried she would get away from him. And Lillian was worried that she wouldn't.

What about Jake?

Had he escaped the men? She wished Jimmy would have asked about him. But obviously she was the one they'd been after, and her bounty hunter had just gotten in the way.

"You aren't going to shoot me," she said. Or he

would have already done it. She wrapped her fingers around the door handle and popped it open.

And the gun cocked. "I will shoot you," he promised.

"You heard Mr. Kuipers," she said. "He wants you to bring me to him."

"He won't mind if I shoot you first," he said.

"But you don't want to."

"I don't," he admitted. "But I don't want to die. And if I let you get away, Kuipers will kill me for certain."

"He will anyway," she said. "He's not going to leave any witnesses to all these crimes he's committed. Why do you think he wants me dead?"

The guy said nothing now. She'd obviously made him think. Or maybe he was beginning to lose consciousness. The others had left him behind because he was hurt. How badly?

"You need medical attention," she said sympathetically. And all that sympathy wasn't feigned. She hated to see anyone in pain. So she offered, "I can drive you to the hospital."

He snorted. "Give it up, lady. I'm not falling for any of your tricks."

"I'm not trying to trick you." She knew how that felt—to be deceived.

Jake had taught her that.

And she'd learned another lesson when she'd trusted someone else with that flash drive. She should have brought it directly to her lawyer—no, to a judge—herself.

But she hadn't exactly legally obtained it or the information on it. She'd been worried that she might be charged with breaking and entering. She'd worried that it might not even be admissible in court. But she'd trusted her lawyer to try.

When would she stop trusting the wrong people?

Her baby kicked, and her belly shifted against the steering wheel. She flinched and sucked in a breath.

"What is it?" the guy asked.

"The baby," she murmured as she rubbed her belly. "I might be going into labor." It was a lie. Even though she hadn't had any contractions yet, she knew they would be far more painful than the baby's kicks. But she couldn't have any contractions yet. It would be way too soon for her baby to be born.

The guy cursed and murmured, "They better hurry up." He peered through the open front window into the woods.

And Lillian took the opportunity to push open the driver's door and run. But as she ran, shots rang out behind her. She flinched with the report of each shot, waiting for the bullet to strike her, to tear into her flesh.

Then she fell and she didn't know if she had been hit or if she'd just stumbled. But her knees hit the asphalt hard before she fell forward. And she couldn't get back up.

I've got her. She walked right up to the van and climbed inside with me.

Jake had been close enough to the guy Jimmy had called to overhear their conversation. And he'd been close enough to take out that man, wrapping his arm around his neck and squeezing until the man passed out.

Jake hadn't wanted him to alert his buddies that Lillian had been captured. He wanted to get to the van before the rest of them did. But as the shots rang out in the woods, he knew he was too late. Either that man must have regained consciousness or someone had spotted him.

But those shots weren't that loud, so they couldn't have been that close to him. They sounded as if they were coming from the road.

From the van into which Lillian had unsuspectingly climbed—probably in order to hot-wire it like she'd tried to hot-wire his truck?

Damn it!

He ran toward the road, heedless of the branches slapping across his face and arms. He didn't give a damn about himself. But if something had happened to Lillian…

If she'd been shot…

Or worse.

He didn't know what the hell he'd do.

The shots died down ahead of him. But they began to ring out behind him, the bullets rustling the trees around him. He felt the whizz of one close to his ear.

The other men had heard the shots, too, and had come running. And shooting.

Ducking low, Jake rushed forward toward the road. He circled around the van and found two bodies lying on the pavement. One body, a long one, was right next to the van, blood pooling beneath it.

He grabbed the weapon from the man's outstretched hand and tucked it into his waistband. The other person had made it farther, to the shoulder on the opposite side of the road. She lay half on the pavement, half in the underbrush off the shoulder, her hair lying across the branches.

"Are you hit?" he asked her as he ran toward her.

She whimpered. "No, I'm stuck." And she tugged, but her hair was tangled in those briar branches. Tears streamed from the corners of her eyes as she struggled to free herself.

"We've got to go!" he said as he wrapped his hand around her arm and jerked her to her feet.

She cried out as her hair came free, leaving several strands behind in the briars.

Jake turned back toward the van. Shots rang out from the woods. He positioned himself between her and the men firing at them. Then he lifted his weapon and squeezed off several shots in the direction of the woods and those men. He hoped his barrage of bullets provided enough cover as he tugged Lillian over the unconscious man and pushed her through the open driver's door. Then he stepped inside the van and swung the door shut behind him.

"The keys are in the ignition," she said.

That was why she'd gotten right into the van. She'd been trying to escape. And he figured it wasn't just those men she'd hoped to elude but him, as well.

He turned the key and the engine roared to life, along with more shots from the woods. He pushed her low as the window in the passenger's door shattered. Another bullet whizzed past his head.

Too close.

He'd been lucky so far, with all the shots fired at him, that no bullets had hit him yet. But his luck was eventually bound to run out.

"Stay down!" he yelled as he slammed the transmission into Drive, pressed on the accelerator and shot forward. The men rushed from the woods, firing wildly.

But he couldn't duck like she was or he wouldn't be able to see where he was driving. But he wouldn't be able to do that if he was dead, either.

And those bullets were getting closer and closer to striking their target.

Him...

Unable to sleep, Donny had parked himself in front of the TV in the living room of the place he'd found to lay low. He felt even lower as he recognized the cottage in front of which news crews were filming a breaking report.

"Shots were fired at this deserted beachfront home tonight."

Grandma's house.

Of course that was where Lillian would have gone, where she would have felt safe.

But she hadn't been safe there.

Apparently, she'd been in so much more danger than he'd realized. Why hadn't he helped her?

Was it too late now?

"The shooters escaped before police arrived at the scene," the reporter continued, but his face piqued with interest as he listened to whatever someone was saying through his earpiece. "Further calls to 911 indicate that there was a car chase not far from here and more reports of shots being fired. When police responded, they discovered a casualty in the road along with another body in the woods."

Donny shuddered as regret and fear overwhelmed him. It was too late for him to do the right thing now.
They'd killed her.
Or had he?

Chapter 7

She was dead. Lillian knew it from the look of fury on Jake's face. If Tom Kuipers didn't kill her, Jake might. And after what he'd gone through that night, she couldn't really blame him.

Of course, he hadn't had to come after her in the first place. If he hadn't, the gunmen wouldn't have followed him to Gran's cottage. They wouldn't have shot it up. They wouldn't have shot at him.

But because he had been shot at, concern squeezed her heart and had her pulse racing. "Did you get hit?" she asked him.

Wind rushed through the van, blowing over his handsome face. He was so damn good-looking, his features perfectly chiseled. The wind pushed back his thick black hair, which he'd always worn a little longer than conventional. With his hair away from his face, she noticed the trail of blood. It ran from his temple and trickled off his jaw onto his chest.

"Oh, my God," she murmured in fear and dread, "you did get hit."

She tried to rise up from the floorboards, but the speed of the van—and the girth and weight of her belly—glued her to the ground.

"Stay down," he warned her.

"You lost them," she said.

He had to have lost them. Since he had the keys to the van, they'd had no way to follow them but on foot. Unless one of those men had been taught to hot-wire a car like her brother Dave had taught her.

Because it was a distinct possibility, she didn't try to rise from the floor again.

"I think I lost them," Jake said. "But I didn't think I was being followed to the cottage, either."

She cared less about that at the moment than she cared about him. Not that she cared about him.

But she didn't want anyone to be hurt, especially because of her. "Did you get hit?" she asked again.

He lifted his fingers to where the blood dribbled from his face. "Just a scratch," he murmured. "Probably from a branch in the woods."

She expelled a slight breath of relief. "Not a bullet."

He didn't confirm that, just shrugged.

"The man in the road." She shuddered as she remembered stepping over his body to get into the van the second time. Sure, he'd been shooting at her, but even then she hadn't wanted him to die. And he'd certainly looked dead.

"He might have just been unconscious," Jake said.

"I must have hit him when I fired back at the van earlier. Or hell, he could have been hit at the cottage."

Fortunately for her, Jimmy had been injured so badly that his shots had gone wild instead of hitting her. Unless he hadn't really wanted to hit her. But the exertion of just firing those shots and getting out of the van must have been too much for him. Hopefully, he'd just lost consciousness from the pain. But Lillian worried it was worse than that.

"I'll call it in," Jake said.

When he reached for his phone, she managed to jump up and grab it from his hand. "You can't," she said. And she felt bad, but surely other people in the area would have reported all the gunfire.

"I need to file a report," Jake said.

"But if you do, you'll have to bring me in," she said.

"Yeah…" He glanced over at her. "That was my whole point of finding you."

Of course it was. He wouldn't have come looking for her if there hadn't been a bounty on her head. For the past eight months, she'd heard nothing from him. He'd never once tried to contact her—proving to her further that she had been nothing but a means to an end for him.

A way to apprehend her family.

Except that her dad and oldest brother no longer considered her family. They blamed her for Jake duping her and catching them. That was fine, though. She blamed herself, too, for being such a fool to fall for him.

That was the reason she was mad at him, for mak-

ing her fall for him when he'd only been using her.
That was what hurt.

Much worse than her family disowning her. If
she'd listened to Gran, she would have disowned
them long ago. Gran had warned her that the Davies men were nothing but trouble and would cause
her pain, just like they had her poor mother.

She felt a twinge of pain now as she remembered
losing her mother the way she had, to that sudden
heart attack. But Lillian didn't believe it had really
been sudden. Her heart had been under attack for
years from all the grief her husband and sons caused
her.

Maybe it was good that Mama was gone and didn't
know Lillian had been arrested now, too. But unlike
the majority of her family, Lillian had not committed
a crime. At least she hadn't committed the crime for
which she'd been arrested. But she had failed to show
up for court, which was breaking a law.

"You can't bring me in," Lillian told Jake. "You
must see now how much danger I'm in."

"You'll be safe in jail," he assured her. "Which
is where you belong since you skipped your court
date."

"I won't be safe in jail," she said. She doubted
she would be safe anywhere since she had no one
she could trust. Despite him saving her from those
men firing at her, she still couldn't trust Jake to protect her, especially since it sounded as if he had no
desire to help her, only to collect the bounty on her.
But maybe he would protect their child. "And neither will your baby."

His hands jerked the wheel and she fell onto the

passenger's seat and knocked her shoulder against the door. The wind blowing through the windshield tangled her hair across her face, so she couldn't see his. She couldn't see how he'd reacted to the news.

And he said nothing.

She doubted her revelation, that he was about to become a father, had swayed him. He still probably fully intended to bring her to jail. And if Mr. Kuipers had gotten to her legal aid lawyer, he could probably get to jail inmates or even some of the guards.

The man wanted her dead. She doubted he would stop trying until she was.

Jake should have brought her to jail. Or at least called the damn police and let them know what was going on...

If the guy he'd left lying in the street was dead from a bullet fired from Jake's weapon, he'd killed him in self-defense. If that wasn't clear, Jake was going to become a wanted fugitive himself. But hell, he would almost rather be a fugitive than what she had claimed he was: a father, the father of her baby...

No.

It wasn't possible.

They had used protection every time they'd had sex. Hadn't they? He did remember once waking up with her lips on his chest before she'd slid them lower.

And he'd lost all control as the need to be inside her body—joined with her—had overwhelmed him. She'd fit him so perfectly, had always been so warm and wet. And the way her inner muscles had felt convulsing around him as she'd found her release.

No. He hadn't used a condom that once. But it only took once.

"Where are we?" she asked when he stopped the van.

She peered through the open front window at the garage in to which he'd pulled the stolen vehicle. He had needed to stash it somewhere it wouldn't be seen. He was certain there was probably an APB out on it—if anyone had managed to take down the license plate number back at the cottage or while it had been trying to run his truck off the road.

"It's not jail," he assured her, because there were some jails where officers would pull in to a garage before releasing the suspects from their vehicles. It cut down on the chance of them escaping, like she had briefly escaped him in the woods. "At least not yet."

She turned back to him, her blue eyes wide with surprise. "Why not?"

She must have thought she hadn't talked him out of bringing her in. Was that why she'd claimed that baby was his? To manipulate him?

Probably. The baby couldn't be his. They had only had sex that one time without protection. She'd just broken up with someone before they'd met. Maybe it was that guy's baby. Or maybe there had been some-one after Jake.

He had no idea how far along she might be. He didn't know anything about pregnant women or babies.

"I brought you here because I want to talk to you," he told her.

She released a ragged sigh. "Thank you."

"Don't thank me," he said and warned her, "I'm still bringing you in."

"Then you'll be killing me and our baby," she said, and she ran her palms over her belly as she leaned back in the passenger's seat.

He sucked in a breath at her blatant manipulation. "Don't try to use your kid to manipulate me," he said. "That baby's not mine."

It couldn't be—for the baby's sake more than Jake's. This kid had been dealt a bad enough hand with the Davies family's DNA. It would be a lot better off if it didn't have his, too.

She sighed again, but this sigh was full of frustration. "You're right," she said as she continued to move her hands over her belly. "This baby isn't yours."

A twinge of pain squeezed his heart, but it couldn't have been disappointment. At least not disappointment that the baby wasn't his. Maybe he was just disappointed that he'd been right about her, that she wasn't the woman he'd thought she was eight months ago. "I'm surprised you're admitting you lied."

But since she was a liar, she was probably a thief as well. He should have brought her straight to jail. Or called the police back in the woods.

But there hadn't really been time to call then. He'd been too busy trying to stay alive and keep her alive. And then he'd wanted to find out why someone wanted her dead.

"This baby isn't yours," she said, but her voice sounded funny now, like she was trying to convince herself as much as she was him. "He or she is just mine."

Now the frustration was all his. She wasn't making any sense. But then nothing about tonight had—from those men shooting at them to someone ordering her death.

"What's really going on, Lillian?" he asked. But he didn't know why he bothered. Would he be able to trust anything she told him? She was obviously as big of a liar and manipulator as the rest of her disreputable family. But she was more dangerous than any member of her criminal family—because she was so damn beautiful.

Too beautiful to resist…even when he knew he should. That he had to…and not just for the bounty he'd get off her but for his life.

Then she reached out and touched his face, skimming her fingertips along the cut near his temple before tracing them down the dried trickle of blood to his jaw.

His pulse quickened, and a sensation raced over his skin from her touch. Every time she'd touched him, she had affected him like this, had had him tensing with desire for her. There was just something about her, something that got inside him and wrapped around his heart, squeezing it tightly.

Nobody had ever affected him like Lillian Davies had. And despite her arrest, that obviously hadn't changed. He still wanted her, even though he knew he couldn't trust her. She was definitely playing him. To escape from him? Or to convince him to help her?

"Are you sure you weren't hit?" she asked.

He felt as if the color had drained from his face, as if he was on the verge of passing out. But that was from her touching him, not from getting hurt.

He assured her, "I wasn't shot."

Which was something of a miracle, considering

all the bullets that had been fired at him that evening. She was going to get him killed.

"Then you must have hit your head," she said, "and hard, if you aren't able to figure out yet that someone wants me dead."

"Oh, I have no doubt about that," he admitted. He'd overheard Jimmy's phone call to his colleague. "I know someone wants you dead."

"Then you know that I'm innocent," she said matter-of-factly.

He shook his head—because it was not a matter of fact to him. "Explain to me—how does that prove your innocence?"

"Why would my boss want me dead if I was guilty?"

"Because you stole money from him," Jake said, and he'd made his voice sound as straightforward as hers had.

It seemed obvious to him now. Her boss was apparently one of those people who chose to take justice into his own hands—probably especially since she'd skipped bail and her court date and was trying to elude the authorities. He didn't trust the courts to deliver justice or to get his money back, so he'd taken it all into his own hands.

"I didn't steal that money!" she hotly denied.

So vehemently that he felt a niggling doubt. Could she be telling the truth?

She's a Davies, he reminded himself. They lie, cheat and steal. It was the family business.

She had once denounced that business to him and had sworn she would never be a part of it. But she'd only told him that after she'd brought him to meet her grandmother and the old woman had disparaged the Davieses. Until then, Lillian had said nothing about her family despite all his efforts to get her to talk. She'd acted as if she was ashamed of them and what they'd done.

That was another thing Jake had found he had in common with her. That, and the loss of their mothers. Maybe that was why he'd thought he was falling for her, because they'd seemed to share so many experiences—bad and good. But then, what must have been shortly after they'd broken up, she had been arrested for embezzlement. And he was no thief.

"If you didn't steal that money," he asked, "why would your boss want you dead?"

"Because I can prove that he is the one who really stole it," she replied.

Jake snorted. "From himself?"

"From the company," she said. "He's not the only one with ownership in it. He might actually not have *any* ownership in it."

And that doubt niggled at him again. Now she was beginning to make sense, or at least provide a plausible excuse for the charges against her.

"His wife and her father have controlling interest," she continued. "Tom Kuipers is just the CFO."

Which gave him access to the funds and control over Lillian since she was an accountant. Kuipers could have set up Lillian to take the fall for his theft.

"But if he framed you, why does he want you dead?" he asked. "Why wouldn't he just send you to prison? Why risk a murder charge?"

"I have a flash drive of files I downloaded that proves his guilt," Lillian said.

Now his brow furrowed as doubts rushed in but these doubts were with her again. "If you really have solid evidence that you're innocent, you could have gotten the charges against you dropped. All you had to do was give it to the police or the prosecutor."

"I gave it to my lawyer," she said. "I thought she would take care of that for me. I thought she would take it to the police, the prosecutor or at least the judge."

Those doubts swirled now in his head and his gut. "She didn't?"

Lillian looked away from him, through the open front window of the van in which they were still sitting. Then she sighed and said, "She claims she never got it."

"That's convenient," he said, letting his skepticism slip back into his voice.

She shook her head. "It's convenient for Tom Kuipers," she said. "Not for me. He must have paid her off."

"So if he has the flash drive, why would he still be after you?" Jake asked.

Now nothing was making sense anymore, including him. He should have just brought her to the police department, then made an official report regarding everything that had happened. His relationship with the police department was already shaky at best. They didn't appreciate bounty hunters and the methods some of them employed. Those shootings, and his part in them, would only make things worse for Jake.

But what if she was telling the truth, not just about her innocence but about his baby?

She was in danger; she wasn't lying about that.

And because she was in danger, so was her unborn child. Even if the baby wasn't his, Jake felt a responsibility to protect it—and Lillian.

He had to find out what the truth really was. He only hoped he didn't get arrested or killed while he tried to find out.

Maybe he should have just given up, but he'd seen the news…and he had a horrible inkling that Jake was somehow involved. So Seymour pressed Jake's contact on his cell screen and called him again.

If Jake had been part of the shooting and that car chase and those casualties, he wouldn't have been able to answer his phone when Seymour had tried calling him earlier.

But now…

If he didn't answer now, it was probably because he was one of those two casualties.

Seymour's heart pounded fast and hard. He didn't want to lose his best bounty hunter.

The O'Hanigans were good. But even those three brothers combined weren't quite as good as Jake.

Nobody was.

Jake seemed to take every bounty personally. It wasn't just a job to him. It was like he was on a mission.

And a man like that, who took things too seriously, was bound to wind up dead in this business. Seymour hadn't needed that phone call warning to know his own days were numbered. And Jake probably didn't need a warning now, either—not if he'd been involved with what was all over the news.

"What!"

Jake's shout startled Seymour into dropping the

cell phone on his desk. He was still at work. Hell, he lived at work. He had nothing else.

Like Jake…

No family. No life outside of the job.

Maybe that was why Jake was his favorite bounty hunter. They had so much in common, except for Jake being more than a foot higher and a hell of a lot younger and better looking.

He fumbled on his desk and grabbed up his cell, wincing as he noticed the crack across the glass. "Jake, where the hell have you been? I've been trying to call you."

"I know," Jake said. "You've been blowing up my damn phone. Why?"

"I wanted you to know that somebody called me about Lillian Davies," he said, and that chill chased over his skin again, making him shiver.

"She just missed her court date," Jake said. "What's the rush to bring her in?"

"This person doesn't want us to bring her in," Seymour replied. "This person doesn't want Lillian Davies going to court."

He waited for Jake to jump to the same conclusion he initially had, that it was one of her family. But Jake said nothing. Something must have made him consider that someone else might not want her brought to jail.

"Whoever it was pretty much threatened me to back off," Seymour continued. And that wasn't like a Davies. They were crooks, but they weren't thugs. The robbery Don and Dave had committed, and for which they were serving time, they'd used airsoft guns—not real weapons. They definitely hadn't been firing any of those shots tonight. "He advised me that my life was more important than my money."

He snorted at that again. That was another reason he knew it wasn't a Davies who'd called him. The Davies family knew how important his money was to him, which was why he'd always sent Jake after them.

Jake cursed, but Seymour doubted it was because the bounty hunter was outraged that he had been threatened. More than likely he was worried about Lillian Davies, confirming Seymour's suspicion that the pretty blonde meant more to Jake than he was willing to admit.

Or maybe he wasn't even aware of how much she meant to him. And that worried Seymour. He didn't want Jake getting killed over her.

"What the hell's going on?" he asked Jake.

Such a long silence followed that Seymour wondered if the connection had been lost. Or if something had happened to Jake already.

Someone had threatened Seymour for sending a bounty hunter after her. They were damn well going to threaten the bounty hunter, too. Maybe they would even kill him to stop him from bringing her back.

Chapter 8

She was in danger. Jake already knew that. He'd been in danger because of her. And apparently he wouldn't be out of danger until she was dead. Or at least out of his custody.

So he should have brought her to jail. Instead, he'd brought her to one of the safe houses he'd set up after leaving the US Marshals. His job with the US Marshals had been dangerous, and he'd needed a place to go in case anyone ever came after him seeking vengeance.

Since that had happened—a few times—he'd kept the place. He also used it as a haven to recharge. He'd used it a lot over the past eight months because guilt over how he'd treated Lillian had weighed on him. That guilt hadn't lessened until yesterday when Seymour had told him about her arrest.

But had she been framed?

He wasn't sure what the hell was going on, so he'd lied to the bail bondsman and told him that he hadn't apprehended her yet. Tuttle would have wanted her brought in right away. He was more concerned about getting back his money than he was about the threat to his life.

Who'd called him?

Tom Kuipers?

The guy was a threat. To Lillian…

Jake stared at the closed door to the bathroom. She'd been in there a while—showering, changing.

He hoped. The bathroom had no window, though, so she wouldn't have been able to escape. There was only a vent to the roof and, with as pregnant as she was, he doubted she would be able to slip through that.

But just to be sure, he stepped closer to the door and listened. Then, when he didn't hear anything, he rapped his knuckles against the solid wood. The house was small but tough—everything was reinforced so if someone came after him, they wouldn't easily get to him. Lillian could lock herself in that bathroom and keep him out. But then she'd be trapping herself inside the small space, and how long could a pregnant woman survive without food?

He knocked again and called out, "Lillian?"

The knob rattled, then turned. When she opened the door, her face was flushed and he suspected it wasn't just from the steam of the shower. The vent cover was a little askew, as if she'd tried taking it down.

"Yes?" she asked.

He narrowed his eyes and studied her flushed face.

She was beautiful, maybe even more so pregnant than she'd been before. Her blue eyes sparkled, and her silky skin had a definite glow to it.

He wanted to skim his fingers along her cheek. But he curled them into his palm so that he wouldn't touch her. Because he knew what happened once he touched her…

Eight months ago, he had never intended to take things as far as they'd gone with her. He'd only wanted to get close to her to get information on her family. He had never intended to become intimate with her.

But once he'd touched her…

He'd been unable to resist her.

But he had to now. Their lives and that unborn baby's life depended on his staying focused and alert. Even if someone had hot-wired his truck, he'd been careful so that the men wouldn't follow him back. And if they'd searched the truck he'd abandoned in the woods, they would find nothing that would lead back to him or to this place.

The truck belonged to someone else—someone who had disappeared a long time ago. That was the one fugitive Jake had never been able to apprehend.

At the moment, though, the only fugitive he cared about was Lillian Davies.

"You were taking a long time in there," he said as he peered around her into the room. It was so small that he could see everything at a glance. "Everything all right?"

Her blue eyes glistened with a hint of tears, but she furiously blinked them back. "It will be once I find that flash drive and prove my innocence."

He really wanted to believe that flash drive existed. "How do you think you're going to do that?"

Her face flushed again. "I—I was going to break into my lawyer's office and search for it."

He reminded her of the words she'd used in the van, "You said she claimed she never got it." That had struck him as odd at the time.

"Yes." She nodded. "That's exactly what she claims."

"But didn't you personally give it to her?" he asked. That was what had been peculiar about what she'd said. Wouldn't she have said, "She claimed I never gave it to her," if she'd given it to her lawyer herself?

Her face flushed again. And he knew.

"If you really had something that important, why would you trust it with anyone else?"

Let alone her family. And he was pretty damn sure that was who she must have asked to deliver it for her. The only one of them she could trust was her grandmother, but he doubted she would have given the elderly woman something that might have potentially put her in danger.

"I—I was scared," she said, and she moved her hands over her belly. She obviously hadn't been scared just for her own safety. "I wanted to get out of town before Mr. Kuipers could get to me."

"Who?" he asked. "Who did you give it to?" It wasn't like there were many of her family members who weren't in jail or prison, so she hadn't had many options.

Maybe she had given it to her grandmother.

She pursed her lips for a moment, as if she

couldn't get out the name. Then finally she confessed, "Donny. I asked Donny to deliver it for me."

He groaned. Her younger brother wasn't the career criminal the rest of her family was, but he was an idiot. If he hadn't sold it, he'd probably lost it.

"Donny is a sweetheart," she said in defense of her younger brother. "He would never do anything that would hurt me."

But after Jake had apprehended her dad and oldest brother at her apartment, the rest of her family had turned on her. They wouldn't care if she was hurt. They might want her hurt nearly as badly as Tom Kuipers apparently did. And Donny would do whatever his dad and Dave told him to do.

Jake wasn't going to argue with her, though, so he just asked, "Where the hell is he?"

If that flash drive existed, he'd beat it out of her little brother for not turning it over to her lawyer.

"He has an apartment down by the community college," she said. Beaming with pride, she added, "He's been taking some classes."

"They have courses in how to be a criminal?" he asked.

She glared at him. "I know how you feel about my family, but you're wrong about them."

"And so were all the juries of their peers who convicted them?"

Her face flushed a deeper red. "I know some of my family have done bad things, and I never condoned that."

He had to admit that was true. She had never claimed her dad and brother had been framed, like she was claiming for herself. When she'd been so upset with him, she'd said it was because he'd used her, not because he'd taken them off to jail.

"But the only reason you caught them is because they care about me," she said. "They risked coming out of hiding because they wanted to make sure the man Donny told them I was seeing was a good man."

He flushed a bit now, his face getting hot over how he hadn't been good to her. He shouldn't have let her go on believing the lie of who he was. But maybe he'd wanted to believe it, too.

Maybe he'd wanted to be as simple and uncomplicated as he'd led her to believe he was.

"So, no," she said. "I don't think any of them would do anything to hurt me, but especially not Donny."

Jake had been there. He knew how angry they'd been. He snorted again.

"Donny is not like the rest of my family," she insisted. "He has never been arrested."

"That doesn't mean he hasn't committed a crime." Maybe he was actually smarter than Jake had thought. So what the hell had he done with that flash drive?

Her eyes glistened again as if tears had rushed to them. "It's easy for you to be so sanctimonious and self-righteous. You probably came from the perfect family with a mother who baked cookies and a dad who worked hard to support you and your siblings."

"No siblings," he said.

And he wasn't going to talk about his mom and dad. He hadn't done that for years. He glanced down her body, focusing on her belly. And he hoped, for that kid's sake, that he wasn't the baby's father.

The kid would have a better chance in life with the Davies family's DNA than with his. The Davieses were criminals and con artists, but they weren't killers.

Jake had that look on his face again, the one he'd gotten any time Lillian had tried to get him to open up about his family. What were they like? Where was he from?

And just as he had every time she'd asked about his, he turned the conversation back to hers. Of course, he'd done that eight months ago because he'd been trying to apprehend her dad and brother Dave for the armed robbery they'd committed. But what was his excuse now?

He just didn't care enough to share anything of himself—of his life—with her?

"Where is Donny's apartment exactly?" he asked. "Give me the address."

"I'll show you."

He narrowed his dark eyes and stared down at her.

"What?" she asked. "Why do you look so suspicious?"

"I don't trust you."

She flinched. "I can say the same thing," she reminded him. "I don't trust you, either. That's why we need to stick together."

Or she doubted he would really search for the flash drive at all. She didn't think he even believed that it existed. It was as if he wanted to think the worst of her. Maybe that would ease his conscience over deceiving her eight months ago.

But she doubted he even had a conscience.

He uttered a ragged sigh. "You're right. You

proved in the woods that I can't trust you. The minute I turn my back, you're going to try to take off." He pointed toward the bathroom and the vent she'd pulled off and then tried to jam back up. "Couldn't make it through there?"

Her face heated up again. And she touched her belly. She should have known without even removing the vent that there was no way she would have fit through that hole. If she'd tried, she would have been stuck like Pooh Bear in Rabbit's hole.

And while they were baggy, she couldn't even blame his clothes for making her look bigger than she was. She was just big—with his baby.

He'd given her some clothes to wear—an old T-shirt of his and a pair of sweats. The sweats were so long that they were bunched up from her ankles to her knees, which was how long the T-shirt hung.

No wonder he wasn't looking at her like he had once—like he wanted her. Instead, he looked at her with suspicion, like she was actually the criminal Mr. Kuipers had framed her to be. She needed that flash drive. Once she had that, maybe she could prove to Jake that she was innocent. Although proving anything to Jake should have been the least of her concerns.

She needed to prove her innocence to the police and to the prosecutor.

He sighed. "It doesn't matter. I know that I can't let you out of my sight, not until I bring you to jail."

She sucked in a breath. How could he still want to turn her in?

Because he didn't trust her any more than she did him.

But at least he'd given her a reprieve. That wouldn't last, though, if she couldn't produce the proof she'd promised she had.

What the hell had Donny done with it?

She'd tried calling him—several times—since talking to her lawyer. His phone must have been shut off because it had gone directly to his voice mail. And he hadn't returned any of her frantic messages.

She'd gone by his apartment, too. But it had been dark with mail overflowing the box. He hadn't been there in a while, either. Had something happened to him?

If it had, it was her fault. Jake was right. She shouldn't have given him that flash drive—because giving him that had probably put him in danger.

And she couldn't help but think that she was putting Jake in danger, too, by asking him to help her find it. She stared up at him and asked the question that had been bothering her, "Why are you helping me?"

"I'm not sure that I am," he said.

"Because you're not sure the flash drive exists." She'd heard the doubt in his deep voice and had seen it in his dark eyes. He wasn't sure he should believe her. "That makes me wonder even more why you're helping me look for it then."

He lifted his broad shoulders in a slight shrug. His chest, beneath his thin black shirt, rippled with the movement. He was so muscular.

He replied, "Maybe I feel like I owe you one."

She forced her gaze from his chest and shoulders to focus on his face. But that was just as distracting. He was so damn handsome. No wonder she hadn't been able to resist him eight months ago, especially when he'd turned on the charm.

"You are doing this to ease your conscience," she said. And although she was relieved that he had one, she didn't feel any less resentful over how he'd used her.

His face flushed now, nearly as red as hers had over the vent. "I already apologized for that."

An apology that she'd thrown back in his face as he'd carted off her dad and brother to jail. Not that they hadn't deserved to get arrested. She hadn't deserved to get her heart broken, though.

"For using me?" she said as all her resentment came rushing out. "For tricking me into betraying my family?"

"I just wanted to get close to you to get information about them," he said.

She rubbed her palms over her belly. "You certainly got close." The baby shifted beneath her touch.

"I thought you said it wasn't mine."

That wasn't what she'd meant when she'd told him the baby was only hers, but maybe it was better he believed he wasn't the father. She would never trust Jake not to hurt their child like he'd hurt her.

"He or she is mine," she repeated. And she would be enough for the baby, if she could stay out of prison.

His dark eyes narrowed and he leaned down, staring into her face. She felt her skin flush with heat again.

"If it is mine, would you tell me?" he asked.

She had told him—in the van—but she didn't want to remind him of that now.

"If it is mine, you would have told me months

ago," he persisted. "Because that would have been the right thing to do."

"Like you'd know what the right thing to do is," she murmured.

"I do know the right thing," he said. "Bringing fugitives to justice."

"By whatever means necessary?"

"I never meant to hurt you," he said.

He had no idea how badly he'd hurt her. She had fallen in love with him and when she'd found out everything had been a lie, her heart had shattered.

She blinked, fighting back the tears that stung her eyes. She didn't want him to know how much she'd cared, how much she'd loved him. But then she hadn't loved him; she'd loved the man he'd pretended to be, not the real Jake Howard. Hell, he hadn't even told her his real name.

She hadn't found out what his real name was until her dad and brother had asked why the hell she was dating Jake Howard. That Jake Howard…the notoriously ruthless bounty hunter.

But he hadn't seemed ruthless to her when they'd met. And he didn't seem ruthless now as he gently cupped her cheek in his palm and tipped her face up to his. "I never meant for things to go as far as they did between us," he said, and there was sincerity and regret in his dark eyes. "I just couldn't…"

"Couldn't what?" she asked.

"Resist you," he murmured just before he covered her mouth with his.

She reached out to push him away, but as his lips moved over hers, she clutched her fingers in his shirt and tugged him closer. She hadn't been able to resist him, either—then or now.

"What the hell happened?" he demanded to know. Tom had shown up at the warehouse, gun in hand, ready to put a bullet in Lillian Davies's brain, but he had no one to shoot now. Unless he turned on his men...

And he was mad enough to start firing.

But if he did that, he would have to hire more people to track down that slippery bitch. "How the hell could she have escaped?"

"That guy," one of the men replied, and he gestured at the truck he'd pulled into the garage. "The one who showed up in this..."

"Why the hell isn't he dead, too?" Was he some kind of pseudo-Rambo? "How did one man and a pregnant woman escape all of you?" Disgust overwhelmed him. Of course, there were two less of them now, two casualties left behind.

But those men wouldn't be traced back to Tom. These guys weren't on the payroll like Lillian Davies had been. Some of the other guys were, though.

The ones he had sitting on places where she might show up. Fortunately, he hadn't put all his confidence in this group of misfits. He pointed to the truck. "Tear it apart. Find out who this guy is and where the hell he is."

If he was a bounty hunter, like Tom had initially thought, wouldn't he have brought her back to jail already? Tom had someone inside in the department, someone he'd paid to notify him if she was apprehended.

She hadn't been yet.

So where the hell had she gone?

His phone vibrated, and he pulled it out of his pocket. "Yeah?"

"She showed up here, at her brother's place," his chief of security said.

And Tom breathed a sigh of relief.

"She's not alone, though," the man added.

His relief was short-lived. "Take that guy out right away!"

"Who is he?"

"I don't know, and I don't care. I just want him dead!" Almost as much as he wanted her dead. This guy was beginning to cause him almost as much trouble as she had.

How the hell had he underestimated Lillian Davies so much? He'd thought she was sweet and naive and the perfect patsy since she came from a family of bumbling criminals. Nobody would believe her over him.

Unless she actually had proof.

"But don't kill her," Tom said. "Bring her back to me in the warehouse."

He still wanted to kill her himself, right after he made damn sure no flash drive existed. His grasp tightened on his gun. He couldn't wait to pull the trigger and put a bullet in her brain.

Chapter 9

Jake could taste her yet—on his lips, on his tongue. Just as he'd told her, she was impossible to resist. Even now, knowing that she could be a criminal just like the rest of her family, he was still attracted to her.

Was she still attracted to him? She'd kissed him back for a long moment before she'd pushed him away from her. Had she just been playing him, though? Using her silky lips and sweet kisses to get him to agree to hunt for this flash drive.

He really hoped the thing existed. He hoped she could prove her innocence. But he wasn't entirely sure he wanted to be wrong about her or right.

If she was exactly the woman she'd seemed to be eight months ago, he had treated her horribly. And if she wasn't...

A twinge struck his heart. Then he was still disappointed. Disappointed that what they'd had—however brief—hadn't been real.

"This is it," she said again as she pointed at the apartment building.

A chill chased down Jake's back, making the skin tingle between his shoulder blades. Something wasn't right about this.

He glanced through the windshield. This car had one. It had been parked in the garage next to the stall into which he'd pulled that shot-up van. He hoped this one didn't get shot up. It was his vintage Chevrolet Nova he had restored a few years ago.

Maybe he shouldn't have driven it tonight. But while the Davieses were criminals, none of them were particularly dangerous. When her dad and brother had committed their last robbery, they'd been armed with airsoft guns. Because they had conned the bank teller into believing their weapons were real, though, they'd been charged with armed robbery. They were lucky they hadn't gotten shot with real guns.

The way they'd yelled at Lillian for betraying them when Jake had apprehended them, he'd wanted to shoot them himself then. If Lillian had had any inkling that he was a bounty hunter, she never would have brought him anywhere near her family. Not that she'd known where they were or that she'd been harboring them. Their showing up at her place had been a complete surprise to her in more ways than one. She'd said she didn't condone anything they'd done.

But she loved them regardless.

But the way they'd turned on her…

Jake doubted they felt the same. So why had she trusted her younger brother with the flash drive?

Why would she trust any of her family?

"You really gave the only proof of your innocence to your younger brother?" he asked. And he didn't bother hiding his skepticism.

She flinched. "I know you don't think much of my family."

"They break the law," he reminded her. And despite her claims of innocence, she might have broken the law, as well.

She flinched again. "Not Donny. He's a good kid."

"He's still a Davies."

"So am I," she said. Then she rubbed her palms over her belly. "So is this baby…"

His baby?

He needed to know. But he wasn't certain he could believe anything she told him. If that flash drive existed, though, if she was telling the truth about that, maybe he could trust her again, like he had all those months ago when he'd started falling for her.

"Okay," he said, gearing himself up to face another member of her family.

None of them had taken his apprehending them well. In addition to her oldest and youngest brothers, there were a couple more in the middle and a couple of uncles and male cousins, too, who had all already been in trouble with the law. Well, except for her younger brother. But if she really had given that flash drive to Donny and he'd done nothing with it to help her, then he was in trouble with Jake.

"Let's go talk to Donny." Before he opened the door, he reached for his holster and drew his weapon.

Lillian reached across the console and grabbed his arm. "You won't need that." She shivered. "Please, put the gun away."

He shook his head. He wasn't sure if he needed it for Donny, but somehow he instinctively knew that he needed it. "After tonight, you can say that?"

She drew in a shuddery breath. "You're right." And she closed her fingers around the passenger's door handle.

"No," he said. "You should stay in the car."

"After tonight, you can say that?" she asked, tossing his words back at him.

He had always loved that sassy sense of humor of hers. She'd made him laugh like no one else ever had. Even now, a grin tugged at his lips, but he fought it. He couldn't let her influence him. But it was already too late. He shouldn't have kissed her because now he couldn't wait to kiss her again.

Why did she get to him like no one else ever had? What was it about Lillian Davies that appealed to him on every level? Emotional, physical...

"Okay," he said. "But you need to stick close to me. Wait until I come around the car."

She patted her belly again. "You don't think I can get over the console?"

"I know you can move fast," he said.

She'd moved too fast earlier that night and had slipped away from him more than once, nearly getting herself and him killed. He had to make sure she didn't slip away again.

He pushed open his door and turned back to tell her, "Wait for me."

And as he said that, he noticed the car parked

across the street. Two dark shadows sat inside it. And then they were no longer inside as they opened their doors and raised their weapons.

"Get down!" he shouted at her just as the shots rang out. He hoped she'd ducked in time as bullets shattered the back window and whizzed past his head. He hunched down, too, to avoid getting shot.

But the shots weren't coming just from that car but from behind him, as well, from the apartment she'd pointed out as Donny's.

Had she set him up?

Was this an ambush to kill off Jake and enable her to escape him? If so, he had a horrible feeling that it just might work.

Lillian proved just how fast she could get over the console when she jumped across it into the driver's seat. Then she turned the keys he'd left in the ignition this time and backed out.

Jake rushed around the front bumper and jerked open the passenger's door just as she'd hoped he would. But he looked at her as if he thought she was the one firing the shots at them. More rang out, pinging off the inside of the vehicle since the back window had already shattered.

With the car in reverse, Lillian jammed on the accelerator, propelling the vehicle out of the apartment parking lot, across the street and into the car from which the men were firing. Those weren't the only shots ringing out, however, since the front window was cracked. The rest of the glass hadn't shattered, though. It had just cracked neatly across, and Lillian could see beneath that hairline fracture as she slammed the car into Drive and tore off down the street, the tires squealing against the asphalt.

"Are you trying to kill me?" Jake asked as his shoulder banged into the passenger's door and his head bumped against the roof.

"I'm trying to get us the hell out of here," she said. "And to make sure we aren't followed." She glanced out the back window at the wreckage of the car she'd hit. The front tire on the driver's side was leaning toward the road. She'd broken the axle. There was no way the men could follow them in that vehicle. So she eased her foot slightly off the accelerator. But her heart continued to race with the fear she'd felt as those shots had rung out.

Jake was looking behind them, too, down the barrel of the gun he had pointed that way. But the men were too far behind them now to be able to hit, even if they were still trying to fire at them. So he pulled his weapon to his side, but he didn't holster it.

"Pull over!" he shouted.

"What's wrong?" she asked.

"Pull over," he repeated, his voice deep and rumbly with anger.

Shaking in reaction now, she steered the car to the curb. She would gladly turn over the driving to him. He reached across the console and pulled the keys from the ignition before opening his door and walking around the hood.

He had every reason to be angry over getting shot at again and over what had happened to his car. It really was—or had been—a very nice vehicle. Instead of getting out the driver's door he'd already jerked open, she crawled over the console again and settled into the passenger's seat.

He said nothing as he started the car and pulled away from the curb. And Lillian had to ask again, "Where are you taking me?"

"I should take you straight to jail," he replied, and a muscle twitched in his cheek. He was clenching his jaw. It looked rigid, as she studied his profile.

Why was he so damn good-looking?

It wasn't fair. She wanted to hate him for how he'd used her. She wanted to…

But as angry as she was with him, she was still attracted to him. That kiss had her lips tingling yet. And her pulse had already been racing before the shooting had started because she'd wanted him to kiss her again.

Why was he so angry with her now? He couldn't think she'd had anything to do with the shooting. But maybe he'd misconstrued why she'd jumped into the driver's seat and started the car.

"I wasn't trying to escape," she told him. "I was trying to get us the hell out of there."

"Out of your setup?" he asked.

"What?"

He shook his head as if he couldn't even form words he was so angry or so disgusted. "I can't believe I fell for it…again."

"What?" she repeated. And how did he mean again? Had he ever fallen for her?

She'd thought so eight months ago. She'd thought he'd come to care about her as much as she had him, that the feelings as well as the undeniable attraction was mutual. But he'd only been playing her.

"I don't understand."

And she didn't—any of it.

He snorted. "You don't understand how I keep surviving?"

She wasn't sure how they had been so lucky that they kept escaping unharmed. But she didn't want to jinx them by mentioning that. "I don't understand why you're so mad...*at me*."

"You lured me here to get shot at," he said. "So yeah, I'm pissed."

"I didn't!" she shouted back in protest. "Those men must have followed us."

"Nobody followed us," he said.

"You thought that before."

"I was extra vigilant this time," he said. "That car was already parked on the street when we arrived. But those weren't the only people shooting at us. There were shots coming from your brother's apartment."

Shots from his apartment? She tensed as fear swept over her again. But this time she wasn't afraid for herself. She hadn't considered every possibility for why that flash drive hadn't shown up at her lawyer's. What if something had happened to Donny once she'd given it to him?

"Did you call him when you were in the bathroom?" he asked. "Is that what took you so long in there?"

He'd already guessed what she'd been doing in there, trying to get her big belly through a small vent. He undoubtedly thought she was an even bigger idiot than he probably already had since she'd fallen for his Prince Charming act all those months ago.

"I tried calling Donny," she admitted. "But he didn't pick up, just like he hasn't every time I've tried calling since I gave him that flash drive." Her voice cracked with fear as she thought of how those gunmen must have been inside his apartment. Before, she'd been afraid that he might have betrayed her. Now she was afraid that she'd betrayed him by putting him in mortal danger. Was her brother dead? Was that why he hadn't returned any of her voice-mail messages?

"Do you think something happened to him?"

"Yes," Jake replied with no sympathy. "I think he pissed off the wrong people."

She wasn't sure now if he was talking about those gunmen or himself.

"Donny wasn't the one firing at you," she said. "He doesn't even own a gun." But now she wished that he had one—not to have fired at Jake but so that he could have protected himself. "Oh, my God, what have I done?"

Had she gotten her brother killed? The horrific thought had sobs bubbling hysterically out of her. She buried her face in her hands, but she couldn't muffle them.

The rest of her family hated her because she had gotten involved with Jake. But for Donny…

He was the only one who'd understood that she hadn't purposely betrayed anyone. He was the only one who'd still been speaking to her. Now he could be gone.

Along with the grief, guilt overwhelmed her for the doubts she'd had. She might not have voiced them like Jake had, but she'd wondered if her brother had done something else with the flash drive other than giving it to her lawyer. She'd worried that he might have seen it as an opportunity to make some money the way the rest of their family did—illegally. Like extortion. Or blackmail.

She had worried that she shouldn't have trusted him. Now it was apparent that he never should have trusted her. Giving him that flash drive had put a target on his back, just like she had one on hers.

The car stopped, but she was so distraught it barely registered that they were no longer moving. Maybe Jake had brought her to jail. And if he had, at the moment it was the least of her concerns.

The passenger's door opened, and he reached for her. But instead of dragging her out, he pulled her against him, and his strong arms wrapped tightly around her as if he was trying to hold her together.

But she doubted that even Jake was strong enough to manage that. If she'd put her brother in danger…

If she'd caused his death…

She wouldn't have to worry about her family ever forgiving her. She would never forgive herself.

The phone vibrating on his desktop jerked Seymour awake. He must have dozed off, as he often did, in his chair. It didn't look like much, with the duct-tape patches, but it was comfortable. He glanced at the cell and saw Jake's contact popping up.

He stabbed at the accept button and said, "You better be calling because you have her!"

A long silence was his reply.

So long that he prodded, "Jake?"

Had someone else gotten hold of the bounty hunter's phone?

"Is that you?" he asked. "Are you there?"

"I'm here," Jake finally answered.

And Seymour expelled a breath of relief. "Are you all right?"

"No," Jake replied with a ragged sigh. "I'm getting damn sick of getting shot at."

"There's been another shoot-out?" Jake had admitted that he'd been involved in those earlier ones when he'd looked for Lillian at her grandmother's cottage. He'd claimed she wasn't there, though.

"Yes, at her brother's apartment," Jake replied.

He must have been looking for her there. It made sense that he would check in with all her relatives and known associates to see if any of them were harboring her. That was how Jake must have gotten to know her before, when he'd been looking for her father and oldest brother.

So who had been shooting at him? Her brother? Or whoever else didn't want her brought in?

Jake continued, "I need you to check out Donny Davies for me."

"Don? He's behind bars."

"Not Senior," Jake replied. "Don Junior."

"So you think he was the one shooting at you? Or was she?" How dangerous was this woman?

She'd seemed so sweet and innocent. Seymour never would have guessed she would skip bail and cause so much trouble. But Jake had known...

Seymour reached for his keyboard and pulled up his databases. Shaking his head, he murmured, "I don't see anything outstanding or otherwise for Donald Davies Junior."

"What about a death certificate?"

"Not yet," Seymour said, "but if you just shot him, he'd still be in the morgue." The River City morgue was usually backlogged for the actual autopsy, let alone the paperwork that went along with one. "The death certificate wouldn't have been recorded yet."

Jake's breath rattled the phone as he expelled a sigh of frustration. "I'll check with the morgue."

Did he think he'd killed Donny Davies? Or did he think someone else had?

Seymour reached for the remote for the TV mounted on the wall across from his desk. He turned on the set to another news report of shots fired across the city. The address was the same as the one on his computer monitor, the one for the last known whereabouts of Donny Davies Junior.

This was getting serious. The news crew at the scene reported that the River City Police Department was not issuing any statements at this time. Was that because they had no information? Or because they wanted to apprehend all the parties involved?

Jake was involved. Had he talked to the police at all? Seymour suspected that he hadn't or he would have asked them the questions he'd just asked him.

"Jake—"

The dial tone emanated from Seymour's phone. Jake had hung up on him.

What the hell was going on?

Shootings?

Casualties?

Jake was probably going to wind up in the morgue,

too, if he wasn't careful. And Seymour had a feeling when it came to Lillian Davies, Jake was too distracted to be as careful as he needed to be in order to survive.

It wasn't until now that he realized Jake had never answered his first question. Did he have her?

And if he did, why the hell hadn't he brought her in yet?

Chapter 10

The door creaked open and Lillian stepped out of the bathroom. The space doubled as a laundry room, and she must have taken her clothes from the dryer because she was dressed in her maternity blouse and torn leggings again. Instead of being flushed like it had been before, her beautiful face was deathly pale. She must have overheard his call to the morgue.

"Is he…" Her voice cracked with emotion, and she couldn't even finish her question.

Jake felt a twinge in his heart, like something was squeezing it. He shook his head. At least her brother wasn't in the morgue, but that didn't mean Donny wasn't dead. Some bodies were never found.

"I never should have given him that flash drive," she murmured.

As he had in the garage, Jake closed his arms around her. Her body trembled in his embrace.

"You trusted him," he said. That had been her real mistake—to trust any member of her family but her grandmother. But at eighty-nine, her grandmother was too old and too fragile to involve in any of this danger.

Lillian tensed and tugged free of him. "I still do," she said. "What happened at his apartment..."

"Us nearly getting killed?" *Again.*

"That proves his innocence," she insisted. "The lawyer must have told Tom Kuipers about the flash drive."

Or Donny himself had.

"He must think Donny has another copy of it," she said. "That's why those gunmen were at his place."

Jake would rather believe that than Lillian setting him up, which had been his first thought when those shots had rung out. But now that his temper had cooled, he didn't believe she'd staged an ambush. She wouldn't have risked her own life and her baby's life. And those bullets had been flying so wildly that she could have easily been hit, too.

He tightened his arms around her. His job was to bring her in to the authorities, but his conscience wouldn't allow him to do that until he knew for certain that she and her unborn baby would be safe.

"You really think Kuipers got to your lawyer somehow?" he asked. This man was far more dangerous and perhaps more powerful than Jake had initially considered.

Her chin bumped against his chest as she nodded vigorously. "Yes, Tom Kuipers is evil," she said. "And he has a lot of money. All that money he claims I stole from the company."

Jake couldn't rule out her claims until he'd investigated them more. And until he'd done that, he couldn't turn her over to the authorities.

"I'll check out your lawyer," he said.

She eased back and peered up at his face. Her beautiful face was stained with tears, which welled yet in her eyes. "You will?"

She seemed stunned that he believed her. She wasn't the only one. Not that Jake necessarily believed her. But he had no proof that she was or wasn't lying. And until he had that, he could make no assumptions.

"Yes."

She released a shuddery breath that sounded like relief. "Thank you." She stepped back farther as if she expected him to do that now.

"I need access to the US Marshals' database," he said. He could pull up records through them that he, on his own, or the bail bondsman couldn't access.

She glanced at the clock on the living room wall, which was awash in sunlight now. Despite being in the city, the house sat between two empty lots. The houses on those had been abandoned so long that they'd been demolished. And before anyone else could build on them, Jake had bought those lots so he could keep the perimeter around the house safe, as well.

He still wasn't certain how they had survived the night with all those people shooting at them. But he was glad that they'd made it back here where he could protect her.

She asked, "Are the offices open yet?"

"Yes." They never really closed.

"Then why are you waiting?"

Because he couldn't bring a fugitive into the offices of the US Marshals. "I can't leave you here."

"You said nobody could find us here," she reminded him. "It's safe."

"It is, but only if you'll stay here." And he didn't think he could trust her to do that. Hell, despite the doubts he was starting to have, he still couldn't trust her.

She paused and nibbled on her bottom lip. And he wanted to nibble on it, as well. Maybe she wasn't the liar he was worrying she was—because she hadn't automatically lied to him and promised she would stay put.

Instead, she held her silence as she stared up at him, as if trying to gauge whether or not she should trust him. After what he'd done eight months ago, he understood her hesitation. But if he'd been honest with her from the beginning, Don and Dave would probably still be on the loose. And she never would have let Jake get close to her, to kiss her, to touch her…

"I was just doing my job then," he said. "Your dad and your brother Dave are dangerous fugitives."

She shook her head, and her blond hair swirled then settled around her thin shoulders. "Dangerous?" She sniffed. "They've never used real guns."

"They robbed a bank," he said. "You condone that?"

She shook her head again. "I told you that I've never condoned what they do. I know they broke the law and…" Obviously, she couldn't bring herself to admit the rest of it.

So Jake continued for her, "And they needed to be apprehended, so they could go to jail."

"What about me?" she asked.

"You're a fugitive now," he said. But he suspected she might only be dangerous to him—if he fell for her again.

She was a fugitive. Lillian couldn't argue that right now. She had been arrested, and she'd missed her court date. But she hadn't been convicted, and she wouldn't be if the prosecutor or judge was able to see the files she'd downloaded to that flash drive.

She needed to find it. But even before she'd spent the night getting shot at and chased around, she'd been exhausted. Now she fought to keep her eyes open. "I'm not dangerous," she told him.

He touched the scratch on his temple. "I'm not so sure about that."

"I didn't do that," she protested. She hadn't even slapped him, despite wanting to really, really badly.

How could he have used her like he had? Why had he made her fall for him as hard as she had for it all to have just been a lie?

"Those men aren't after me," he said. "Unless you sent them after me."

She sucked in a breath. "I'm not dangerous," she insisted. "And I don't want anyone getting hurt—not even Kuipers's men." And if Donny had been hurt because of her…

No. She couldn't think about that. She would rather believe that he had betrayed her than that she'd caused him harm.

A muscle twitched in Jake's cheek. "I had to fire back at those men," he said.

She nodded. "I know. They were shooting at you.

If you hadn't fired back…" They would have killed Jake. And that thought filled her with horror. She had convinced herself that she'd never wanted to see him again.

But if she couldn't…

If he was no longer alive…

Pain squeezed her heart, and she reached out and slid her arms around his waist. His body was so tall—so muscular. So strong and warm.

He wrapped his arms around her, as well, and settled his chin against the top of her head. "And I couldn't let them take you," he said.

"Thank you," she said. She wasn't sure if she had thanked him, really thanked him. He hadn't had to help her like he had been. He could have just let the bad men take her.

But then he wouldn't get his bounty.

She pulled back and wrapped her arms around herself now, trying to get a grip. She couldn't let herself fall for him again—out of gratitude. This time she knew exactly who and what he was.

A bounty hunter.

Of course, he wouldn't collect that bounty if he didn't bring her to jail. And he hadn't done that yet.

Would he? If he found the flash drive, if she proved her innocence…?

"I couldn't let them hurt you," he said. He stared down at her so intently that she shivered. But she wasn't cold; heat flashed through her.

How was she still so attracted to him? Maybe because she knew that he'd just been doing his job. She hadn't been mad, though, that he'd apprehended her dad and brother—just that he'd used her to do it.

"What about you?" she asked. "Are you going to hurt me? Again?"

He expelled a ragged breath. "Damn, Lillian, I never meant..."

To break her heart? To destroy her? To get her pregnant? Hadn't he known how hard she would fall for him?

But then how could he have known what she had never guessed? She'd been so careful all her twenty-five years. She'd protected her heart just like Gran had advised her, so that she wouldn't wind up like her mother, falling for the wrong man and living with criminals.

Jake wasn't a criminal, though. He hunted them. He'd hunted down her.

She was a criminal, unless that flash drive could be found to prove her innocence. She cared less about herself and that evidence than her brother at the moment. She should have brought it to the lawyer herself. She never should have gotten anyone else involved in the mess that her life had become. "What do you think happened to Donny?"

Jake shrugged. "I don't know. Your family is good at hiding."

"Not me..." she murmured.

He had found her easily enough.

"You're not good at hiding," he agreed. "So when I leave here to look for that flash drive and Donny, you better not go anywhere—because I will find you. And then I will take you straight to jail."

Ever since she was a little girl, whenever she got too tired or anxious, she got silly. So these words slipped out almost against her will: "No passing Go? No collecting two hundred dollars?"

He shook his head again, but he was grinning now. And she remembered why she'd fallen for him. This was the Jake she had loved—the grinning one who'd laughed at all her corny jokes, with whom she'd had so much fun.

And so much passion…

The grin slid away from his handsome face, his eyes getting even darker and more intense as he stared down at her. "Damn it," he murmured.

And she knew he felt it, too: the attraction that she hadn't been able to fight eight months ago. Not that she'd tried all that hard. She wanted to fight harder this time. She wanted to fight it and win.

But when he leaned down and lowered his mouth to hers, she didn't push him back. Like the last time he'd kissed her, she clutched her fingers in the soft material of his T-shirt and tugged him closer. Then she rose up on tiptoe and kissed him back. He groaned and deepened the kiss, pushing his tongue between her lips.

Heat flashed through her as her pulse quickened with passion and excitement. It had been so long since she'd felt like this—since she'd felt anything but fear.

She felt the fear, too, along with the excitement and passion. This fear wasn't just over going to jail or even getting killed. She was afraid that she might fall for Jake all over again.

He moved his hands from her shoulders down to

the curve of her hips. But he couldn't pull her any closer, not with her belly between them.

The baby kicked. And Jake must have felt it, too, because he jerked back.

"Did I hurt him?"

Him.

He'd instinctively called him that, too.

If she was carrying a boy, Jake would have a son. She would have a son, and that thought increased her fear. Her baby was half Davies, too, and the Davies men had not turned out well.

Except maybe for Donny…

"Is he okay?" Jake asked again.

Lillian took Jake's hand and placed it over her belly. "He's fine. He's just very active."

Jake stared down at her, a look of awe on his handsome face as the baby moved beneath his touch. "Very active," he murmured.

"Yeah, given my luck, he probably has ADHD," she said.

And he chuckled, though Lillian hadn't entirely been joking.

"He does move a lot," Jake said.

The baby was even more active now, with Jake's hand lying on her belly. Like the rest of Jake Howard, his hand was so big and strong but still could be so gentle. She remembered the way he'd touched her, and she wanted that touch again.

She wanted Jake.

"You need to go to bed," he said.

Her heart jumped and her pulse raced away. But

then she realized he'd said *you* and not *we*. He didn't want to go to bed with her.

His hand not on her belly cupped her cheek and he skimmed his thumb across the skin below her eye. "You look exhausted."

She was—so exhausted that she couldn't fight the rush of disappointment that swept over her. Tears welled in her eyes, and she was too tired to fight them back. So one trailed down her face and over his thumb.

"Lillian…?"

She closed her eyes, so she couldn't see him. Because just looking at him aroused her, made her want him so badly that she could forget how painfully he'd broken her heart and her trust. He, obviously, didn't want her the same way anymore.

"What's wrong?" he asked. Then he snorted derisively at himself. "Of course, I know what's wrong."

"Everything," she murmured. But then her baby kicked, reminding her of the one thing that was right in her life. Having this child, having Jake's child…

He gently brushed away her tears and touched his lips to her forehead. And his tenderness caused a whole new rush of tears.

He was making it so hard for her to hang on to her anger and resentment of him. He was making it so hard for her to remember that she needed to hate him now—not love him.

"You need some rest," he said. Then he easily swung her up in his arms as if she weighed no more than she had before—when he used to carry her so effortlessly. But then, when he'd carried her to bed, he'd joined her. Now he carried her into a bedroom and just laid her on the bed.

But he stared down at her. Even with her eyes closed, she could feel his gaze on her. So she looked up at him, and one of her fears bubbled out. "Am I that repulsive to you?"

"What?" His brow furrowed with confusion. "What are you talking about?"

She touched her belly. "I'm huge. So I'm probably a huge turnoff."

He laughed.

And the laugh struck her like a slap, making more tears spring forth along with a gasp.

He sat on the bed next to her. "Lillian! I thought you were joking."

She touched her belly again. "This is no joke."

"I know," he said. "How do you not know?"

Now she furrowed her brow as confusion overwhelmed her. She was too tired. She couldn't understand him. But then she'd struggled to understand him eight months ago when she'd found out he was just using her. She'd failed to understand how he could be so ruthless about his job that he'd had no regard for her feelings and her heart.

"Know what?" she asked.

"That you're beautiful," he said and a sigh that sounded almost wistful escaped his lips.

She shook her head. "No, not now…" She knew what she looked like, that she had big dark circles rimming her eyes, making her face look like a raccoon's, while her body with her big belly made her look like a beached whale.

"More now than ever before," he said. "I never knew what people were talking about when they claimed that pregnant women glow. Now I know. You're...radiant..."

She laughed now. He had to be joking.

But the look on his face was so intense, so sincere, that she believed him. Of course, she'd believed him before—when he'd told her his fake name and job. But he didn't restore old cars for a living, and he wasn't Jacob Williams. Actually, he had restored at least one old car...

But his name—that had been a lie. Wasn't it?

She wondered now—who was the real Jake?

And dare she believe anything he told her?

"If you really think that, why did you pull away from me?" she asked. "Why aren't you in this bed with me?" Instead of sitting so far on the edge of it that he looked like he was about to fall onto the floor?

He groaned, and heat brightened his dark eyes. "I want to," he said. "I want to join you so...badly."

Her heart flipped and she gasped as that heat rushed through her. She wanted to reach out to him. She wanted to drag him into that bed with her.

But he shook his head. "But we can't..."

She knew the reasons. So many reasons why it was a bad idea...

But still she asked, "Why not?"

"I don't want to hurt the baby."

She shook her head. "The doctor said sex won't hurt the baby."

"You asked?" Jake tensed. "Have you been seeing someone?"

Another laugh slipped through her lips, but it sounded high-pitched and a little hysterical. "Yeah, right. Like anyone would want to date me."

"I told you you're even more beautiful—"

She shook her head. "I'm also facing trial for a crime I was framed for," she reminded him. "I've been trying to prove my innocence. So I've been a little busy."

"What about before all that?" he asked. "Were you seeing someone then?"

"Since you?" she asked the question he obviously wanted to but hadn't.

He nodded. "Yeah, since me."

"No," she said. But she didn't want him to think she was still in love with him, even though she was beginning to fear that she was. "After you, I couldn't trust anyone else."

He flinched and moved off the bed. He hadn't fallen. He just stood up and stepped away. "You're not the only one struggling to trust right now," he told her.

And she returned his flinch.

"You've been arrested," he said.

"I told you I was framed."

But he continued as if she hadn't spoken, "You skipped your trial. You're on the run. Why should I trust you?"

"Because *I* never lied to *you*," she said.

"I don't know that for sure," he said. "I don't know that you're telling me the truth now about this flash drive full of evidence. It could just be a ploy."

"A ploy?"

"To get away from me," he said, "so I don't bring you to jail."

"It's not," she insisted, although she was no longer convinced that the flash drive existed. She hoped it—and Donny—had not been destroyed. But it had existed. She'd risked her life once already to get it. "I don't lie."

"If that's true, you're the only Davies who doesn't, then," he said.

And he was right. She probably was the only Davies who didn't lie. So had Donny lied to her when he'd promised he'd bring the flash drive to her lawyer?

Had every man she'd ever loved lied to her?

Tears stung her eyes and her nose. She was too tired to fight them, so she just closed her eyes. And those tears streamed out and trailed down the sides of her face. She heard the catch of his breath. He must have seen those tears. Her lids were so heavy now that she couldn't lift them again—even when she felt the brush of his lips across her forehead.

And he whispered, "Be here when I get back."

She was too tired to try to escape from him now. So she only nodded and let herself drift off to sleep. Or maybe she'd already been asleep and this whole ordeal had just been a nightmare. Not just the arrest but Jake not being the man he'd told her he was.

Maybe when she awakened, she would be lying in the arms of Jacob Williams—her head against his chest, his heart beating slow and steady against her ear.

* * *

Tom Kuipers expelled a ragged sigh of relief. "So you managed to follow them?"

"Yes, they took out one vehicle, but they didn't know we had another parked in the apartment lot. We followed. We have eyes on them now."

"I want more than eyes on them," he said. "I want them dead."

"That hasn't been easy to manage," his chief of security, Archie Wells, said. "We don't know yet who the hell this guy is or what he's doing."

"What?" Tom prodded as Archie trailed off. "What's he doing?"

Archie replied, "He's leaving the house."

Tom's chest swelled with hope. "Alone? Is he alone?"

Archie waited a few seconds as if he was checking before replying, "Yes."

"Then let him leave," Tom said. For now...

"I thought you wanted him dead."

"I want her more," Tom said. "Since her bodyguard is gone, get her and bring her back to me."

If he had to, he would torture the truth out of her about that damn flash drive. He had to make sure no evidence existed that proved what he'd done. He could not go to prison; that was not part of his plans.

"What about the guy?" Archie asked.

"Have someone wait for him to come back," Tom ordered. "And take him out then."

Tom clicked off the phone and kicked his feet up on his desk. Relief flooded him. Finally, the plan had gotten back on track. It would all be over soon. And he wouldn't have to worry about anyone ever figuring out the truth.

As long as that damn flash drive didn't really exist. If it did…

He would have to find it and destroy it, just like he intended to destroy Lillian Davies.

Chapter 11

What the hell was wrong with him?

Jake's chest felt tight, like something was pressing on his lungs. He struggled to draw a breath. But it wasn't just his chest that ached; his heart hurt, too. Like someone was squeezing it.

Lillian.

She'd had that effect on him before—eight months ago. But he'd thought he was smarter now. That, given her arrest, he would be more cautious. He had no proof that anything she was saying was the truth.

So how had he let her get to him again?

She had him so distracted that he must not have noticed someone tailing them from her brother's apartment. He saw that tail now, as he backed out of the garage. This wasn't a neighborhood where people parked on the street and sat in their vehicles.

That was why he'd chosen it for his safe house. So he could easily spot the people who didn't belong. The two guys in the white vehicle didn't belong.

The cargo van looked suspiciously like the shot-up one parked in his garage. Of course, there were a lot of white vans on the road. But two identical ones in the same vicinity that looked like they had probably been leased for the same company. Tom Kuipers's company?

Whatever else she might be lying about, Lillian wasn't lying about how dangerous her former employer was. So if she was telling the truth about that, maybe she was telling the truth about everything else.

"Damn," he murmured.

If she was a liar, he might be able to protect himself. But if she was as honest as he'd once thought she was, he had no protection from her.

But he wasn't the one in danger right now. She was. He had left her alone and unprotected in the house. But he had no doubt she wouldn't be alone long. The men wouldn't be able to easily get inside, but they might be able to coerce her into coming out. They were obviously there for her since no car followed him.

Jake turned the corner and circled around the block. There was an alley behind his house, another way in and out. He had thoroughly researched the location before he'd bought the place, planning for every scenario.

He had not planned for one like this—with a pregnant woman in danger. He had to be careful so that he didn't put her more at risk. But if those men got inside the house, if they got to her…

The place was a fortress.

The locks were unpickable. The doors were steel and so were the jambs. That way they could not be kicked open. The windows were bulletproof glass, which made them impossible to break. Even the walls of the little bungalow were brick, so they couldn't take a chainsaw and cut them down. They would have to drive a tank through the walls to get inside the house.

That was the only reason he'd left her—because he'd thought she would be safe. But while he had taken every safety precaution with the house, he couldn't trust that Lillian wouldn't open the door herself.

She had already tried to escape him twice. What if she had only been faking falling asleep and she tried to leave again and walked right into the clutches of her killers?

His heart racing with fear for her, he stopped the car in the alley and jerked the keys from the ignition. He needed another key that dangled from the ring in his hand. He needed the key for the lock on the gate to the alley, because the fence around the house was impenetrable, too.

His hand shook as he struggled to insert the key in the lock. He had to hurry. He could hear pounding. Someone was trying to kick in the door.

If she opened it before he got there…

She might be dead before he ever had the chance to save her—if the guys started shooting like they had at her grandmother's cottage once they'd stepped through the door.

The thought of her being in that kind of danger

steadied his hand and he easily turned the key, unlocking the solid metal gate. He pushed it open and rushed into the backyard, his weapon drawn.

Someone must have come around the back of the house looking for another way inside because he came under immediate fire. Bullets struck the fence near his head, pinging off the metal. The shots were close.

Ducking low, he raised his weapon and returned fire. He had only seen two guys in the white van parked on the street from the house. But with the number of shots ringing out, he realized now that there were more.

How the hell had he missed seeing them, too? Were they that good or was he that distracted? Since he'd met her, Lillian had become a distraction for him. Eight months ago, after he'd gotten to know her, he'd even considered not going after her fugitive family. But then they'd shown up and recognized him and he'd had no choice.

He had no choice now. He had to get to the house—even if he got shot trying to get there.

Jake had been in some dangerous situations before, but for the first time, he was worried that this one he might not survive.

And if he didn't survive, what were Lillian's chances?

Falling asleep hadn't brought Lillian out of a nightmare but into another one. This dream was so real, it was as if the pounding and the gunfire actually echoed around her. She flinched with the retort of each shot.

And she jerked awake with a scream tearing out of her throat. She couldn't have been asleep for very long. She wasn't at all rested. But of course that might have been because of the dream.

Then she heard more shots ring out, and she knew she hadn't been dreaming at all. The nightmare was real.

What the hell was going on?

Jake couldn't have been gone very long. Was he one of the people shooting? Had he stepped outside his door into another ambush?

She'd had no idea going to her brother's apartment had been walking into a trap. Had Donny been part of that? If he'd gotten a gun, though, it would have been to protect himself.

Not to kill someone. Not even Jake.

Her family did hate him, though.

But while her family consisted of criminals, none of them were killers.

She gasped as a horrific thought occurred to her. Could Jake be dead? But then why wouldn't the firing have stopped?

She wanted to cower under the covers and pretend she was just dreaming. But this was real. Jake was in danger. And so was she.

She couldn't hide and pretend they wouldn't find her. Obviously, they knew where she was if they'd followed her and Jake here from Donny's apartment. So she was the one they were coming for.

She scrambled out of the bed and began to search the bedroom. The room was small and sparsely furnished, like the rest of the house. If this was Jake's home, he didn't have much stuff in it. No artwork or knickknacks. And nothing personal at all—no photos or books. Maybe this was just the safe house he'd told her it was.

But then wouldn't Jake have another weapon stashed in it? He would have more than the one he carried in his holster. Wouldn't he?

Even if Lillian found a gun, she wasn't sure she'd be able to use it. The lessons Gran had given her had been a long time ago. And she hadn't been that good at it, either. The recoil had hurt her wrist and nearly made her drop the heavy weapon. So if she found a gun, she wouldn't be able to outshoot anyone. She would have to outrun them.

Looking down at her big belly, she sighed. While being pregnant was a hindrance, it was also a great motivator. All of her new maternal instincts were screaming at her to protect her baby.

But when the gunfire suddenly died down, she thought only of the baby's father. And her heart lurched with dread.

Was Jake dead?

No. He was too good a shot himself, probably from his years as a US marshal and now as a bounty hunter. The men hadn't hurt him at the cottage, in the woods or at Donny's apartment. How could he die here where he'd assured her they would be safe?

He couldn't.

He couldn't die, not when she was beginning to have all these old feelings for him again. Not when she was beginning to fall for the father of her baby all over.

"Jake." His name escaped her lips on a gasp.

Her pulse pounding, she rushed from the bedroom

into the living room. But she stopped at the front door. If she unlocked the dead bolts and opened it, she might step out into the same ambush that Jake had. She didn't know what to do.

If Jake was gone, she had no one to protect her. If she stepped outside now...

Tears stung her eyes as pain squeezed her heart. Not Jake... He had to be all right. He had to have survived all that gunfire. But if he hadn't...

She couldn't stay here forever. Then the locks clicked, and the doorknob began to turn. She couldn't stay any longer. They were coming for her now. So she turned and ran toward the kitchen. Her hands shook as she fumbled with the locks on the back door.

The front door creaked open just as she turned the last dead bolt on the back one. They had gotten inside. She didn't have long now, not if she hoped to escape with her life.

She jerked open the back door and stepped onto the deck. And as she did, someone lifted her off her feet. But he didn't carry her like Jake had—carefully, gently...

He had wrapped his strong arms around her own, so she couldn't fight him with her fists. She could only scream and kick her legs, struggling to escape.

She couldn't see his face—her back was pressed against his chest. But he was like Jake in that he was big—too big for her to overpower. Too big for her to wrest free of him.

She could not get away.

Jake Howard had lost his damn mind and probably his life, too. Shane O'Hanigan felt a moment's regret over the loss of the other bounty hunter. But not even Jake could have survived that barrage of bullets.

Shane had barely survived himself. And he still wasn't certain about his brothers—until he heard their voices emanating from the two-way radio in his ear.

"All clear," Ryan said.

"The gunmen drove off in that white van," Trick confirmed. "I think at least one of them was hit, maybe both of them."

"What about you two?" he asked. As the oldest, he felt responsible for his brothers—especially since he'd brought them in to the family business with him.

"I'm fine," Ryan said.

"Me, too," his brother Patrick, who they all called Trick, added.

Shane breathed a sigh of relief, which stirred the blond hair of the woman he held in his arms. He knew his brothers were old enough and certainly big enough to take care of themselves. They'd proved it over and over. But still, he worried.

"I've got her," he told his brothers. But she was fighting fiercely to escape him. He grunted as the heel of her foot connected with his shin again. Her struggle distracted him from asking the others about Jake.

Had he survived, as well? Or was he lying dead or bleeding out somewhere in his own yard?

Jake must have forgotten he was a bounty hunter. He'd been acting more like a bodyguard to Lillian Davies. Why else had he brought her here instead of jail?

Had old Jake gone soft because she was pregnant? Shane had noticed that immediately when he'd lifted her and his arms had touched the mound of her belly. He could even feel the baby kick. She must be pretty far along.

Hmm…

Hadn't her dad and oldest brother skipped bail about eight or nine months ago? Jake had brought them in, but it had taken him a few weeks to track them down. Jake never took that long to track down anyone.

But maybe something or someone had distracted him, someone like the pretty blonde struggling in Shane's arms. Was the baby she carried Jake's?

Along with another kick inside her belly, Shane felt a pang of sympathy. But it wasn't his baby she was carrying. So he still intended to bring her to jail. Then he'd collect the bounty for her.

And after he'd cashed the check, he and his brothers would go down to O'Hanigan's pub and raise a pint in a toast to the dearly departed competition.

Poor Jake…

To risk his life for her, he must have fallen for her. And that was what happened when a man fell in love. He lost his damn mind and his life. Love was the only thing that could have made Jake act like such a fool.

Shane was no fool. He would never fall in love. But suddenly he was falling.

It wasn't Lillian Davies who'd brought him down, though. Something had struck him over the head. Pain radiated throughout his skull.

He shouldn't have trusted his brothers to make

sure those gunmen were gone. He should have checked himself. But it was too late now…because everything went black.

Chapter 12

"Is he dead?" Lillian asked as she stared at the prone body of Shane O'Hanigan. Concern darkened her blue eyes and puckered her usually smooth forehead.

Jake shook his head. He'd hit him hard but not hard enough to kill him, especially when the guy was as thickheaded as Shane O'Hanigan.

"Are you okay?" Jake asked.

She had fallen, too, and lay sprawled across Shane's motionless body. Had she been hurt or was the baby hurt?

He dropped to his knees beside her. It had been a risk to knock Shane out like he had. But he'd needed to get a jump on the big bounty hunter or Shane would have had time to fight him. Or alert his even bigger younger brothers.

"I'm okay," she said, but her voice shook with fear. And she didn't try to stand.

So Jake picked her up and carried her off the deck. As he headed across the backyard, he asked, "Why'd you go out the back door?"

Had she been trying to escape?

"Someone was coming in the front," she said, and her voice cracked with the fear she must have felt then.

He should have called out to her. "That was me." He was the one who'd had the keys. But if he'd been shot, someone would have been able to take those keys off him.

He glanced around as he hurried toward the gate.

The O'Hanigans were like the Three Stooges of bounty hunters. They never went anywhere alone. Since Shane was here, then Ryan and Trick had to be nearby, too.

Jake rushed through the gate he'd left open to the alley and helped Lillian into the passenger's side of his battered vehicle.

"Are *you* okay?" she asked as she stared across the console at him.

He nodded as he jammed his key into the ignition and started the car. But before he could drive away, Lillian reached across the console and cupped his face in her palms. She stared at him as if unable to believe that he was real.

"How?" she asked. "I heard all those gunshots…" She shuddered.

He shrugged. But he knew. He probably had the O'Hanigans to thank for helping him survive the gunfight. Their arrival had spooked Kuipers's men into giving up and driving off. They must have thought they were outnumbered then.

But Jake knew the O'Hanigans were not on his side. They had been his rivals for a few years now, mostly thanks to Tuttle playing them off against each other. What the hell had they been doing at his place?

How had they even figured out where it was? Had he told Tuttle before?

He wouldn't have had to for the wily old bail bondsman to figure out where it was, though. Tuttle had a way of finding out stuff no one else had. Jake suspected Tuttle even knew what motivated him to pursue fugitives.

And Jake knew what motivated Tuttle, too, although that was no secret. Money.

He glanced into the rearview mirror as he drove away from his place. Were the O'Hanigans following him? Were Kuipers's men? Even as he kept a vigilant gaze on the road, he grabbed his cell phone from his pocket and punched in Tuttle's contact.

It rang a few times before Tuttle picked up and slowly murmured, "Hello, Jake…"

"You son of a bitch," Jake called him out.

"What?"

"You sent the O'Hanigans after me."

"After her," Tuttle corrected him.

"How did you know I had her?"

"You're not a good liar, Jake," Tuttle admonished him.

Lillian must have been able to hear the other man through the cell because she glanced over at him, as if tempted to chime in that Tuttle was wrong. She thought he was a very good liar. She didn't know he'd been more honest with her than he had been with anyone else in his life.

He was more the man she'd known than the one everyone else thought he was.

"Well, your boys failed," Jake said.

And Tuttle groaned. "Damn it, Jake, you gotta bring her in. Her lawyer's been calling, too, wanting to get her back before the judge."

"Why?" Jake asked. "Does her lawyer have any evidence to help her?"

"Help her what?" Tuttle asked. "She's in big trouble, Jake. You know that."

Unfortunately, he did. He'd nearly gotten killed again protecting her from Kuipers's men. The guy wasn't just pissed off because she'd stolen money from him. This was bigger than that, more self-preservation than just revenge.

Jake was beginning to believe that she was telling him the truth about everything. Maybe even about him being the father of her baby.

She'd only said that once. But after the way he'd reacted, she had probably thought he didn't want to be a father. That wasn't the case—not entirely. It was more like he *shouldn't* be a father.

"I'll bring her to you," Jake offered.

And in the passenger's seat, Lillian gasped.

"But have her lawyer there—in your office," Jake said. "I want to talk to her." He wanted to find out just who the hell was telling the truth here.

"Jake, this is crazy," Tuttle said. "I don't want to get any more involved in this mess than I already am. I just want to get my money back."

"I know," Jake said. It was all about money. Not

just for Tuttle but for Tom Kuipers, too. "And you'll get it back, but on my terms."

Tuttle sighed. "Damn you."

"Get her lawyer in your office within the hour, and I'll bring her to you." He clicked off the phone without waiting for Tuttle to argue any more or to agree. Tuttle wanted his money back. He would meet Jake's terms—terms that Jake had no intention of meeting himself.

He was a better liar than Seymour knew, even though he wasn't the liar Lillian thought he was. Instead of heading toward Tuttle's office, he turned in the opposite direction. It was about damn time he figured out who was telling the truth and who was lying.

Before he got killed...

Just when she'd been starting to trust him again, Jake had betrayed her all over again. Lillian's heart ached with the pain of that betrayal. The old one and the new one.

"How could you?" she murmured. He'd offered her up like some kind of trophy.

Jake chuckled, totally unrepentant. "I guess I'm a better liar than Tuttle thinks I am."

"I know you are," she agreed as her resentment bubbled over. She reached for the door handle. If she wasn't pregnant, she would have jumped out of the car while it was moving. But because she was pregnant, she would have to wait for Jake to stop the car before she jumped out. She couldn't risk the baby, not any more than his life had already been risked. "You've lied to me over and over again."

"I lied to *him*," Jake said as he braked at a red light.

Lillian's fingers curled around the door handle, but she hesitated before opening the door.

"What?" she asked.

"I'm not bringing you to Tuttle's office."

She wasn't sure if she should believe him. She glanced from his face to the traffic light, which was still red. How much more time did she have? Her fingers twitched on the handle. Even if she opened it and ran, he was faster. He would catch her—just like he had in the woods.

"Where are you bringing me?" she asked as the light turned green and he pressed on the gas again.

"The lawyer's office," he said. "We're going to search it for that flash drive."

Relief flooded her. "Thank you."

He shrugged off her gratitude. "Don't get your hopes up," he advised her. "I don't think we'll find it."

Was that because he didn't think it existed? Or he thought her brother had never brought it to the lawyer?

Lillian wasn't certain what to believe, either, when it came to her problems and to Jake. Of course, he was her biggest problem, because she had never gotten over him.

And she was afraid that she never would.

But what if he was lying to her instead of the bail bondsman? Maybe he would have to stop at another red light and she could make her escape then.

He stopped again but not at another traffic light. He pulled into a parking lot, one she didn't recognize.

"This isn't the lawyer's office," she said. The only business she saw was a rental car company.

"We have to ditch the Nova," he said with a sigh of resignation. "It's too recognizable."

And now they had more than Tom Kuipers's men looking for them. They had those other bounty hunters after them. She nodded in agreement.

"Stay here," he said as he pushed open the driver's door. But before he slid out, he grabbed the keys from the ignition. He didn't trust her any more than she did him.

He didn't leave her alone for very long before he was back, driving a gray SUV that he pulled up alongside the Nova. He helped her out of his car and into the rental. She breathed a sigh of appreciation as she settled onto the comfortable seat. It had much more cushion than the old bucket seat in his Nova.

His lips curved into a slight grin. "No appreciation for the old girl?"

She shook her head and gestured toward the windows. "That's not the case," she said. "I have a greater appreciation for intact glass now than I ever had before."

"I thought it was like riding in a convertible," he said, glancing over at his banged-up vehicle. He uttered a ragged sigh. "Maybe I'll make it into one. Might be easier than trying to repair all that damage."

"You really did restore it?" she asked.

He nodded.

And she wondered how much he had actually lied to her. He hadn't lied to her about where he was bringing her, because the next parking lot in to which he pulled was the one she had parked in just the night before when she'd staked out this office.

It wasn't night now, though. Even if her lawyer had left to meet with the bail bondsman, there were other people in the building and a receptionist and coworkers in the lawyer's office.

"How are we going to do this?" she asked.

He hadn't brought her to the bondsman's office. But she was still concerned that she would be caught and brought to jail.

"Don't worry," Jake told her.

Which was an impossible command.

All she had done was worry—for months now. That could not be good for the baby. And it certainly wasn't good for her.

"Trust me," Jake said.

She didn't. She couldn't. But she really had no choice. She needed the evidence that would prove her innocence. She wanted it to be here for so many reasons—one of which was that it would prove Donny's innocence as well as hers. If it was in her lawyer's office, it would prove that her younger brother had not betrayed her.

Jake's plan was so simple that Lillian smiled when he pulled the fire alarm. Once everyone cleared out of the building, they were easily able to search the lawyer's office. The lawyer must have backed up all her records to an online storage provider because there wasn't a single flash drive in the place, let alone the one Lillian had risked her life to get from her former employer.

It was gone.

Her legs began to shake and threatened to fold

beneath her. But when she moved to sit down, Jake grasped her arm and tugged her toward the door.

"We have to get out of here," he said, just as the alarm stopped wailing.

Obviously, it had been identified as false. They wouldn't have much time to escape. So she hurried with Jake toward the back stairwell, which led down to the parking lot. Another alarm sounded as they slipped out the emergency exit. Jake rushed her toward the SUV and barely waited until she shut the door before he peeled out of the lot.

Lillian felt sick with disappointment. She'd counted on the lawyer having the flash drive. But if Tom Kuipers had bought it from her, then he would have it in his possession.

Or maybe it had never gotten to her lawyer.

Had Donny betrayed her?

Lillian was beginning to think that he had.

And if every man she trusted betrayed her, it was only a matter of time before Jake did again. Was he driving her to the bail bondsman now?

Since they hadn't found the flash drive, he probably didn't believe her that it existed. She'd lost her one chance to prove her innocence to him.

And somehow, proving it to him mattered almost as much as proving it to the authorities. She wanted Jake to know that she was exactly who she'd shown him she was eight months ago. She hadn't lied or deceived him.

She was not a criminal like the rest of her family. But unfortunately, at the moment, she was a fugitive.

Seymour waited until the lawyer walked out of his office before he released the string of profanity he'd

suppressed for the hour and a half that he'd waited
for Jake Howard to show up with Lillian Davies.

But Jake hadn't shown up—alone or with the
beautiful fugitive. Jake had betrayed him.

"Son of a bitch!" he yelled.

"Hey," Shane O'Hanigan said, grimacing as he
stepped into the office. "Can you keep it down?"

"Howard hit him over the head," Ryan added as he
followed his brother inside the small space. The two
dark-haired men were so damn tall and broad that
they barely fit, but then the third brother joined them.

Trick O'Hanigan, bringing up the rear, snorted.
"Shane's getting old and slow, or he would have seen
him coming."

"He should have seen it coming," Ryan agreed.

"He got past the two of you," Shane said.

Usually the O'Hanigans' sibling rivalry amused
Seymour. But not now. Not when the three of them
were making him feel claustrophobic in his own
damn office. He jerked at his already loosened tie.
Usually he didn't bother wearing one with his polyester suit, but he'd dressed up for the lawyer.

Only to be made to look like a fool…

Damn Jake Howard!

"How the hell did that happen?" Seymour demanded to know. "How did Jake get the jump on
the *three* of you?" As he stared up at them, their faces
flushed slightly, making their green eyes look even
brighter. They were all dark haired and green eyed—
looking as much like triplets as individual brothers.

"I thought he was dead," Shane said. "I don't know
how the hell he isn't. But somehow he dodged every

bullet those guys were firing at him." He shook his head. "He must be bulletproof."

"Nobody's bulletproof," Seymour said.

Not even Jake.

But it was probably going to take a bullet to prove that to him.

"We're just damn lucky we didn't get hit in the cross fire," Ryan said. "What the hell's going on, Tuttle? You sent us to pick up a bounty—not get shot at."

Seymour dropped with such force into the chair behind his desk that it rolled back with him and struck the wall. The frames of the pictures on it rattled against the paneling. "I don't know what the hell's going on…"

The lawyer had shed a little light on the situation, though. She had admitted to talking to Lillian Davies before the trial was to start. When she'd told the woman that she had never received some flash drive that was supposed to have been delivered to her, Lillian had gotten upset. Then after that conversation, she hadn't shown up for court.

"That was her lawyer that just left," Seymour said.

Ryan whistled. "She's hot."

Shane snorted and shook his head. "Didn't today teach you anything?"

"Like what?" Ryan asked.

"That women are nothing but trouble," Shane said. "Jake nearly got himself killed today over one."

"He's getting old and slow, too," Trick said with a chuckle.

Trick was the youngest of the O'Hanigans, probably in his twenties yet, so his oldest brother, Shane, and Jake, who were in their early thirties, might have seemed old to him. To Seymour, they were all young men.

Young enough to think they were invincible. Seymour knew better. Nobody was invincible.

"Jake's in love," Shane said with a snort of disgust.

Seymour shivered as that chill raced over him again. The thought had occurred to him already, but he asked Shane, "Why do you say that?"

"She's knocked up," Shane said. "Probably at least eight months along, which would be about how long ago that Jake went after her dad and oldest brother."

Jake had gotten far more involved with Lillian Davies than Seymour had even realized. This was not good. If that baby was Jake's, he would undoubtedly do anything to protect it and Lillian Davies.

"Her lawyer thinks she's innocent," Seymour admitted.

Shane shrugged. "Does that make a difference? Do you not want to bring her in anymore?"

"No," Seymour said. He wasn't going to lose his money—not even over an innocent woman. "But someone obviously doesn't want to give her the chance to prove her innocence."

"So that's why all those guys were shooting at Jake," Ryan said.

"And us," Shane said. "They were shooting at us, too. But not like they were Jake. It's pretty clear somebody wants him dead."

Damn it...

He couldn't lose Jake.

"I need you guys to track him down again," Seymour said. "I need you to bring her in."

Shane shook his head, then grimaced. He must have taken a hard knock to his head.

"Guess your brother is right," Seymour goaded him, "you are getting old and slow."

Shane was probably younger than Jake and certainly more reckless. Seymour doubted that he was refusing to help because he was scared.

"No, this is Jake's bounty," Shane said. "And probably his baby, too."

"He can't do this alone," Seymour said. "I can't lose him. You guys are good, but he's the best."

"Guess we're going to be the best soon," Shane O'Hanigan said, "because it's not looking good for old Jake. If we hadn't shown up when we did, Jake would already be dead."

And Seymour had no doubt the men would try again. Eventually, Jake's luck was going to run out and he would realize he wasn't bulletproof or invincible. But by then, it would be too late.

Chapter 13

"This doesn't look like jail," Lillian said as Jake closed the hotel door behind them. He had rented a suite, but since he'd had to pay cash, it wasn't fancy. But at least it looked clean with freshly vacuumed commercial carpet on the floor and crisp linens on the bed.

As safe houses went, though, it wasn't that safe. Not with walls in common with other rooms and only the one door in and out. But his safe house was no longer safe, either, since it seemed like everybody in the whole damn city knew where it was. Not only had Kuipers's men tailed him to it, but the O'Hanigans knew where it was, too. And after the shooting, it was damn likely that the police were sitting on it now, wanting to figure out what the hell had happened there.

"You thought I was bringing you to jail?" he asked, surprised.

But it was clear from the paleness of her face and the way she trembled that she had been scared that he was. She hadn't tried to talk him out of it, though. There had been no pleading or manipulation. Since they'd left the lawyer's office, she hadn't said anything at all, until now.

"We didn't find the flash drive," she said. "So you probably think I've been lying about it all along."

Not even a Davies could feign the disappointment that had shown on her beautiful face when the flash drive hadn't turned up in her lawyer's office. Tears had welled in her ears, and her bottom lip had appeared to tremble slightly.

"I think you've been lying to yourself," he said.

Her brow furrowed as she stared at him. "About the flash drive? I risked my life breaking into my old office to download those files to it. I didn't make that up."

"I know," he said. And he did. He also flinched at the thought of the risk she had taken—alone—when she'd done that.

"You should have called me," he said.

Her blue eyes widened in surprise. "What?"

"When you got arrested," he said. "You should have called me."

"Why?" she asked. "So you could talk Seymour Tuttle out of posting my bail? He told me that you made him swear to never bail out another Davies."

Tuttle had broken that promise, so Jake didn't feel too bad about breaking his to bring her to the bail bondsman's office. "Yeah, I did tell him that…"

She sucked in a breath like he'd punched her.

"But I didn't think *you* would ever get arrested," he said. At first, he'd been so shocked. Then after that, he had been both disappointed and relieved. He still couldn't decide if he would rather she had lied to him eight months ago or now…

"You actually would have helped me," she asked, her blond brows arching with skepticism, "had I reached out to you?"

He nodded. He wouldn't have been able to help himself, just like he couldn't now.

"Why didn't you ever contact me?" she asked, and her voice cracked with emotion.

And he knew that he'd made a mistake—maybe an even bigger mistake than in deceiving her in the first place. But she'd been so furious with him…

"You told me that you hated me," he said. "I didn't think your feelings were going to change." She'd been very upset with him—so upset with him that he'd doubted he could have done or said anything to change her feelings toward him.

But if he'd helped her then…

"That's why you didn't call me," he said, answering his own question. "Because you hate me."

"And you hate all Davieses," she said.

"I don't hate them," he said.

And he didn't. Bringing them to justice had never been personal for him. At least not any more personal than it had been with any other fugitive…until he'd gotten involved with Lillian. Then it had gotten too personal.

"But I don't trust them," he admitted. "And neither should you."

She made a noise with her lips and stammered, "But I—I am one."

"That's why you should have known better," he maintained. "And that's how you've been lying to yourself. You must know that your brother never brought that flash drive to your lawyer."

She gasped now. But she shook her head, too, denying what she had to know was the truth. "No. He knows how important it was to me that he bring it to her. He knew that my freedom depended on it..." Her voice cracked, and her trembling body began to shake even more.

He stepped closer and wrapped his arms around her, trying to hold her together.

But she bristled in his embrace, and instead of clutching him, her hands pushed against his chest. "No, you're wrong. You're wrong!"

He was afraid the only thing he'd been wrong about was her. And that was just recently. Despite her arrest, she wasn't like the rest of her family. She was no criminal. She was as good and sweet as he'd initially thought she was.

And because she was, he was in danger of falling for her all over again. That danger was far greater than even Tom Kuipers's men shooting at him—because it was clear she would never return his feelings as she once had.

She hated him every bit as much as she had eight months ago when she'd thought he was using her. And even if she was able to stop hating him, he doubted that she would ever be able to forgive him or trust him again.

* * *

Jake stumbled back, making Lillian realize how hard she'd been shoving him. He was so big and muscular that she was surprised she had moved him at all. But he didn't look like he'd been shoved. He looked like he'd been struck. The color had drained from his face, leaving his eyes looking so dark and intense.

Had he been hit?

Had someone fired through the door behind them? She reached for him now, running her hands over his chest. And she anxiously asked, "Are you all right?"

He shook his head. "Nooo…"

"What's wrong?"

"I'm sorry," he said. And he said it so heavily, like it had been weighing on his soul and conscience for a long while.

And for the first time since she'd discovered that he'd been lying to her, she believed that he was actually sincere.

"I never meant to hurt you," he said.

Was he talking about the past or the present?

She wasn't sure. And she knew he had no reason to be sorry about the present. He was trying to help her. But like he'd said, she wanted to keep lying to herself. She didn't want to believe that he was right about her brother and that she was wrong.

But what other explanation was there for her lawyer not getting that flash drive?

She closed her eyes, fighting back the flow of tears rushing to them. But they leaked out the corners and streamed down her face.

His arms closed around her, pulling her against his

chest. She didn't push him back this time. Instead, she clung to him. But she wasn't seeking comfort.

Passion rushed through her, overwhelming her like the tears. She reached up and pulled his head down for her kiss. She slid her lips over his, nibbling at them, before deepening the kiss. She stroked his tongue with hers.

And he groaned and clutched her back. "Lillian…"

"You won't hurt the baby," she reminded him. But he would hurt her if he rejected her again.

"You hate me," he reminded her.

She wanted to hate him. Then he wouldn't be able to hurt her again.

"I want you," she said.

It had been so long since she had experienced the pleasure that only he had ever brought her. If she wound up in jail or worse yet—dead—she wanted to feel that pleasure one last time. She kissed him again, nibbling at his lips, on his tongue. Then she implored him, "Jake…"

He groaned again, then swung her up in his arms. Carrying her as if she weighed nothing, he brought her to the bed. And he laid her down again.

She reached up, holding her arms out for him—to tug him down with her, on top of her.

But he resisted.

And she had the horrible feeling that he was just going to tuck her in to sleep as he had earlier that day. He claimed he still thought she was beautiful. So maybe she could seduce him…

She reached for the buttons of her blouse and tugged them free. The pink cotton parted, revealing the swell of her belly before falling away from her bra. Her breasts nearly spilled over the cups; they were so much fuller with her pregnancy than they'd once been.

Jake's eyes darkened as he stared at her. And she could hear him breathing; it was as if he was panting for air. "Lillian…"

"Jake," she parroted. She shrugged off the blouse, then she reached behind her and unclasped her bra. It fell away from her breasts.

And he groaned. Like his apology, it was heavy and sounded as if it had been ripped from his soul. That guttural groan must have been the sound of his control snapping because now he moved. He undressed quickly—only taking time with the holster that he set on the table next to the bed. His clothes he just let drop to the floor until he stood before her, naked and so very obviously aroused.

He hadn't lied. He still found her beautiful. Desirable.

Her heart warmed as her flesh heated, and her blood felt as though it had caught fire, rushing hot through her veins. She found him so beautiful. So desirable…

His skin stretched taut over all his rippling muscles. She wanted to touch him. To taste him…

She reached out for him. But he caught her hand and held it away from him.

"No," he said. "It's been too long. If you touch me, it'll be all over."

Too long? Too long since he'd been with her? Or too long since he had been with anyone at all?

She wanted to ask. But he had leaned down to kiss her. And she didn't care about the past or the future.

She cared only about the present and the pleasure she knew Jake would give her. He took his time kissing her, skimming his lips over and over hers before he deepened the kiss.

His tongue stroked across hers, teasing and tasting her. And she moaned at the exquisite torture.

Then he touched her, running his hands gently over her body—including the swell of her belly. The baby must have been asleep now because there was only a faint flutter of movement. Then Jake cupped her breasts.

A cry of pleasure slipped between her lips. Her breasts were even more sensitive than they'd been before. And they had always been sensitive to his touch. When he flicked his thumbs across her nipples, heat radiated from her core. She wanted him so badly that she whimpered with her desperate need.

"Jake…"

He lowered his head to her breasts and kissed the swollen flesh before closing his lips around one of her nipples. He tugged gently.

And she cried out again at the pleasure. But it wasn't enough, not when she knew he could give her so much more. She reached out and tugged him toward her—toward the bed.

But he shook his head. "I don't want to crush you."

A smile tugged at her lips. "Then I guess I'll have to be on top."

He chuckled because he knew that was no great hardship for her. She had loved being on top, had loved being in control. And in the bedroom, he had had no problem turning over control to her before.

But that was then.

What was now?

Finally, he joined her on the bed, but he lay on his back. She straddled him, guiding his erection inside her. He was so big, but she arched and took him deeper. Her inner muscles already began to convulse as she came at just that first tentative thrust. He moved—but slowly and gently—and she knew he was still concerned about the baby.

And he didn't even really believe that it was his.

Jake was a better man than her family thought he was. A better man than she'd thought he was. Maybe even a better man than he knew he was.

The slow rhythm drove her out of her mind as she came again and again. His name slipped through her lips as she cried out in pleasure.

Then he tensed beneath her. And he came, too.

She eased off him and dropped onto the mattress next to him. And as she had all those months ago when they'd slept together, she settled her head into the nook between his shoulder and his neck and she closed her eyes.

She wasn't sure if she could sleep for fear that the nightmare that was her life would come rushing back to her. But with Jake's heart beating beneath her ear, she was lulled to sleep with a sense of security. He would keep her safe.

From those men…

But he couldn't keep her safe from getting hurt again. Lillian feared it was already too late for that. She was afraid she'd fallen for Jake Howard all over again. Or maybe she'd fallen for him for the first time, because now she knew who he really was.

* * *

"Who the hell is he?" Tom Kuipers demanded to know from his chief of security.

Archie Wells sat in the chair in front of Tom's desk. The two of them having a meeting would raise less suspicion if it took place here rather than in the warehouse during the day.

Archie was probably about Tom's age. But Archie looked it because he'd let his hair go gray, whereas Tom dyed his a chestnut brown. He kept his longer, too, so it would wave. Archie wore his in the same military brush cut he'd worn in the service. He was a former marine or navy SEAL or something.

Until now, Tom had respected him. But he'd let that damn guy and Lillian Davies get away.

Archie shook his head. "I don't know who he is, but I think I know what he is…"

"What?" Tom asked. "A bodyguard?" Lillian Davies probably didn't have the resources to hire one of those, though—even with what Tom had paid for that damn flash drive he'd never received. "A bounty hunter?"

That made more sense. Since she hadn't shown up for court, she'd skipped out on her bail. And the guy who'd bonded her out, Seymour Tuttle, had a reputation for caring only about money. Since he hadn't heeded Tom's threat to let her go, that reputation must have been earned.

The guy would rather die than give up a buck.

"I don't know for sure what he does. But I think he's indestructible," Archie replied. "He's such a damn good shot. And his reflexes and his instincts…" The security chief trailed off with a sigh.

"4 for 4" MINI-SURVEY

We are prepared to **REWARD** you with 2 FREE books and 2 FREE gifts for completing our MINI SURVEY!

FREE
Value Over
$20!

You'll get...

TWO FREE BOOKS & TWO FREE GIFTS

just for participating in our Mini Survey!

Dear Reader,

IT'S A FACT: if you answer 4 quick questions, we'll send you **4 FREE REWARDS!**

I'm not kidding you. As a leading publisher of women's fiction, we value your opinions... and your time. That's why we are prepared to **reward** you handsomely for completing our mini-survey. In fact, we have 4 Free Rewards for you, including 2 free books and 2 free gifts.

As you may have guessed, that's why our mini-survey is called **"4 for 4"**. Answer 4 questions and get 4 Free Rewards. It's that simple!

Thank you for participating in our survey,

Pam Powers

To get your 4 FREE REWARDS:
Complete the survey below and return the insert today to receive 2 FREE BOOKS and 2 FREE GIFTS guaranteed!

"4 for 4" MINI-SURVEY

1 Is reading one of your favorite hobbies?
☐ YES   ☐ NO

2 Do you prefer to read instead of watch TV?
☐ YES   ☐ NO

3 Do you read newspapers and magazines?
☐ YES   ☐ NO

4 Do you enjoy trying new book series with FREE BOOKS?
☐ YES   ☐ NO

YES! I have completed the above Mini-Survey. Please send me my 4 FREE REWARDS (worth over $20 retail). I understand that I am under no obligation to buy anything, as explained on the back of this card.

240/340 HDL GMYJ

FIRST NAME   LAST NAME

ADDRESS

APT.#   CITY

STATE/PROV.   ZIP/POSTAL CODE

READER SERVICE—Here's how it works:

▼ If offer card is missing write to: Reader Service, P.O. Box 1341, Buffalo, NY 14240-8531 or visit www.ReaderService.com ▼

BUSINESS REPLY MAIL
FIRST-CLASS MAIL   PERMIT NO. 717   BUFFALO, NY

POSTAGE WILL BE PAID BY ADDRESSEE

READER SERVICE
PO BOX 1341
BUFFALO NY 14240-8571

NO POSTAGE
NECESSARY
IF MAILED
IN THE
UNITED STATES

And Tom grimaced. "You got a man crush on him?" he asked with disgust.

The chief glared at him. "I have a healthy respect for him."

Tom snorted. He respected few people himself. And this conversation had just ended whatever he'd had for his chief of security.

"And having that respect will probably keep me alive," Archie added. Another man had been shot at the house to which Archie and one of his guards had followed Lillian Davies and her protector.

So that guy was out of commission. The two from the night before were dead. Others had quit. Tom's resources were dwindling. He would have to tap into some more of that money he'd stolen, like he had when he'd bought the damn flash drive.

How could he have been so stupid? He'd paid for something before he'd checked it out. The one that had been dropped in the locker where he'd left the money had been empty. Of course, there might have never been anything on it. Or the real one might still be out there—ready to incriminate him.

He needed to find it and Lillian Davies ASAP. "Killing him will keep you alive," Tom said.

And the chief nodded in understanding. He must have figured out that he wasn't in danger just from the man helping Lillian. He was in danger from Tom, as well.

If Tom didn't get Lillian Davies and that flash drive soon, more people were going to die. And he was going to start killing them himself.

Chapter 14

Over the past eight months, Jake had spent so many nights lying awake in the dark, missing the warmth of Lillian nestled in his arms like she had been every night since that first time they'd made love. She'd fit against him so perfectly, had felt so right lying on him, her body curled against his side.

For a while tonight, he'd had that warmth—that rightness—back. He could taste her yet on his lips, feel the warmth of her body as he'd filled her.

And the pleasure…

It had been every bit as mind-blowing as he'd remembered. And it must have blown his mind or he'd just lost it entirely. How had he fallen asleep?

Knowing the danger she was in, how had he been able to sleep at all?

He jerked awake now. But when he did, he found himself alone in bed. Had he dreamed it all?

Had she never been there?

No. He could smell the scent that was hers alone— like wildflowers and fresh rain. And he could feel her yet, the warmth of her body where she'd lain beside him. The sheets were warm yet, too.

She hadn't been gone long.

Maybe she was just in the bathroom. Didn't pregnant women have to get up all the time?

"Lillian?" he called out.

But the door to the bathroom stood open, no light spilling from it. No sound.

Where the hell had she gone?

Her blouse was no longer lying on the floor. Neither were her pants. And as he fumbled around the clothes he'd dropped to the floor, he discovered that the keys to the rental vehicle were gone, too.

Damn it!

He never should have trusted her. She'd played him, using sex as a way to escape him. How the hell had he fallen for it? Why had he begun to trust her again?

She was every bit the Davies that her dad and brothers were. She was a con and a crook.

With his rental vehicle gone, he had no idea how to track her down—even if he knew where to look. But he jumped out of bed anyway and quickly dressed.

He would hunt her down and catch her—just as he had her brother and her dad. There was only one fugitive who'd ever escaped Jake. And that was probably only because he hadn't really wanted to find him.

He hadn't ever wanted to see him again—because he hadn't trusted himself to bring the fugitive in to the proper authorities. He wouldn't have been able to wait for the man's trial and conviction. Jake would have sentenced him himself and administered his own justice.

That was what he felt like doing with Lillian now. He was furious with her. Not just for playing him but for putting her life at risk.

She knew she was in danger. Why the hell would she have gone out on her own?

And then he knew. She must have figured out where her brother was. Maybe she thought that without Jake along she would have a chance to get through to Donny and get back the flash drive.

Despite how she'd played him tonight, Jake still believed the flash drive existed. He'd seen her disappointment when they hadn't found it in the lawyer's office. But then he'd seen her passion and desire when they'd made love.

And he'd thought he'd seen something else on her face, as well. He'd thought she'd cared about him again.

So what was real and what was the con when it came to Lillian?

Damn it!

He never should have trusted her.

Jake was never going to trust her again. And Lillian didn't blame him. Was she crazy for sneaking out like she had? She hadn't wanted to escape him. Hell, she hadn't wanted to leave him at all. She'd felt so safe and protected lying in his arms. But more than that, she'd felt like she had eight months ago—like she belonged at his side and he at hers.

And that wasn't right. If they were meant to be together, they would have been together. He wouldn't have stayed away the past eight months.

She knew other couples that had broken up and then reunited later. Their new relationships had proven stronger after the separation. They'd appreciated each other more after being apart. But those other couples hadn't had to overcome the lies and broken trust that lay between her and Jake.

But when she'd been thinking of revisiting past relationships, it had dawned on her where Donny was. Of course, his relationship with Katie hadn't ended any better than hers with Jake. But at least Jake had just lied to her. He hadn't cheated like Donny had. At least she didn't think he had.

But she had no idea what had been real back then. She wasn't even sure of her own feelings—since she hadn't known who Jake really was. Her stomach lurched with the horrible thought that he might have been involved with someone else. But when would he have managed to see anyone else?

After their first meeting, they had spent all their free time together. And they'd both made sure they'd had plenty of free time for each other. No. He couldn't have been seeing anyone else back then. Was he now?

When they'd made love, he had said it had been a long time. But for them? Or for him specifically?

She shook her head and focused on the road. This was the way to Katie's, wasn't it? She had been to the young woman's house a couple of times when she had babysat Katie's twins so that the young mother and Donny could go out. Lillian would have tried to look up the address on her phone, but her cell had died some time ago.

Maybe there was a charger in the glove box of the SUV. She pulled it over to the shoulder of the road and reached inside the glove box. All she found were papers, and as she held them into the glow from the streetlamp over the SUV, she spied the name on the papers: Jacob Williams.

Jake had rented the vehicle in the name he'd given her eight months ago. Had he used the alias so that no one would find out he'd rented the SUV? Or was that his real name? A picture of his license was included in the paperwork. It could have been fake, though.

Just like Jake.

He was a fake. She had no idea who or what the real Jake was. Her head pounded, and she wished she had slept instead of lying awake thinking about their relationship. She didn't regret making love with him, though. He made her feel pleasure she hadn't thought possible to feel.

He was an incredible lover. But more than his skill was the connection she felt with him, closer than she had ever felt to anyone else.

"Jake…" She sighed. She blinked against the sting of tears and focused on the street sign at the corner.

This was it.

She'd instinctively driven to the right place. As she glanced down the street, she saw the house, too. It was dark now—like the night. Maybe she had slept a few hours in Jake's arms after all.

It had been daylight when they'd arrived at the hotel. And with spring here, it stayed light out longer now, especially since the time had sprung ahead. But she didn't feel rested. She felt on edge.

And scared…

And it wasn't just because she was here alone. She was scared that she was falling for Jake again.

That was why she had left him behind, sleeping. It wasn't just because she'd been afraid that Donny would run if he saw the bounty hunter. But she suspected he would have if he'd done anything wrong.

And he'd been wrong to not bring that flash drive to her lawyer. How could he have done that to her?

Hell, he would probably run when he saw her, too. If he'd wanted to talk to her, he would have returned at least one of the many, many calls she'd made to him. Maybe he hadn't been able to, though. Just because Jake hadn't found him in a morgue didn't mean Donny wasn't dead.

If he was here, hiding out at his old girlfriend's, he'd better run from Lillian. Because she was going to kill him…

She swung open the driver's door and rushed down the street, then up the steps to the front porch. Up close, the house wasn't as dark as she'd thought. A light glowed inside, so Lillian rang the bell.

Katie must not have been asleep because she quickly jerked open the door, saying, "Did you lose your key?" She stopped when she saw Lillian standing on her porch, and her mouth fell open in shock.

"No, I didn't lose my key," Lillian said. "I lost something else, though. And I think Donny has it."

The young woman tensed and stepped forward, pushing Lillian out more onto the porch rather than allowing her inside. "What are you doing here?"

"Looking for my brother," Lillian said.

The woman shrugged her thin shoulders. She wore just a tank top and boxers, like she had been about to go to bed or she had just gotten up from bed. "I haven't seen Donny in a while." But when she said it, she glanced down as if unable to meet Lillian's gaze.

"I know you're back together," Lillian bluffed.

The woman shook her head, sending her ponytail bobbing back and forth across her shoulders. "No. I can't believe you'd think I would take him back after the way he treated me!"

Lillian thought of making love with Jake, of how much she'd missed him and ached for him despite his lies. If Katie and Donny had had even a small percentage of the passion that Lillian shared with Jake, then she believed Katie would take him back. "Yes."

Katie snickered but it sounded brittle with nerves. "Not a chance…"

"My brother can be charming," Lillian said. He'd gotten her to trust him, and she should have known better. She had known him all his life. Katie had only known him a couple years.

"I'm not the only girl he's charming, though," Katie said. "I never am…"

That was probably the truth. And Katie had slipped up with tense. She wasn't talking in the past anymore. She had definitely been talking to Donny recently.

"Did he mention anything about me?" Lillian asked. "About the trouble I'm in?"

The woman glanced nervously around Lillian, staring at the street. She'd obviously been expecting someone—someone who had a key to let himself into her home. "I don't know what you're talking about," she murmured. "I haven't talked to Donny in a while."

"I don't believe you," Lillian said.

The girl sucked in a breath and looked at Lillian now. "You're calling *me* a liar?"

She had definitely heard about the trouble Lillian was in. But Katie could have just seen it on the news. Just because she knew about it didn't prove that she had been talking to Donny. But Lillian was pretty convinced that she had been.

Katie sniffed and looked down her nose at Lillian. "After what you've done, you shouldn't be acting so lily-white anymore."

And Lillian sucked in a breath now as if the other woman had punched her. That hurt. Her dad and brothers had always called her that—lily-white Lillian. From them, she'd taken it as a term of endearment. But now, she wasn't too sure that they hadn't been mocking and patronizing her.

She had never really felt like part of her family. At least not like part of the Davies side. She'd been her mother's daughter. And Gran's favorite. She blinked back tears, missing her mother all over again.

And Gran. She had to get better. Lillian couldn't lose her, too.

Katie reached out and squeezed her arm. "I'm sorry, Lillian. That was a bitchy thing to say. I know you're in trouble. It's all over the news. You're a fugitive now." She glanced around the street again. "You've got to get out of here."

"Who are you waiting for?" Lillian asked her. "My brother?"

Katie shook her head. "No. You're in trouble, Lillian. And I don't want any trouble."

"Then you shouldn't have gotten involved with my brother again," Lillian said.

Katie didn't bother denying it verbally. She just shook her head again. "You have to leave," she insisted. Putting her hands on Lillian's shoulders, she pushed her back a couple of steps farther from the door. "I can't have you around my kids."

Not all that long ago, she had begged Lillian to babysit the twins and praised her for being so good with them. Of course, now Lillian realized the young mother had probably just been using her— like so many other people had—for free childcare. But at least it had given Lillian practice for when she would become a mother, which was going to be much sooner than she'd planned on becoming one. The baby kicked, hard enough that Lillian gasped and clutched her stomach.

Was that a kick? Or a contraction? The sensation hadn't been in just one spot. It had felt more like a tightening of her stomach than of the baby just moving inside it.

"Are you okay?" Katie asked, alarm in her voice.

Then another alarm echoed Katie's when from somewhere inside the house a child screamed. And another shouted, "There's a man in Timmy's room!"

Katie cursed, but she didn't run for the stairs the way Lillian started to. Instead, she held Lillian back. "It's probably just your stupid brother," she said. "I never should have let him back into my life."

"No, you shouldn't have," Lillian agreed. But she didn't think Katie's kid would have screamed over finding Donny in his bedroom. It had to be someone else. Had one of those men followed Lillian here?

Was he searching for the flash drive she'd given Donny?

Timmy screamed again. And Katie must have realized what Lillian already had. That wasn't Donny in her child's room. If Lillian was smart, she would have run for the SUV and safety. But a kid was in danger probably because of her, so she had to do what she could to help—even if she risked her own life doing it.

The scream reached inside Donny, tearing out of his heart. That was one of Katie's kids screaming. And that was his sister heading up the stairs to that kid.

What the hell had he done?

He'd put Lillian in danger. And now he had brought that danger to his girl and her kids. None of them deserved this—just because of his greed.

He pulled the gun he'd just bought from his pocket. He hadn't had to fill out any paperwork or wait for approval. All he'd had to do was look up one of his older brother Dave's friends.

After watching all the news and seeing his apartment on the latest broadcast, he'd known he would need a gun, that they were coming for him now. He just hadn't expected to have to use it so soon.

It wasn't an airsoft pistol like his dad and Dave had used to rob that bank. This was a real gun.

But Donny knew he could use it, especially when he heard another scream ring out and recognized it as Katie's. This scream was even louder than when she'd caught him in bed with another girl.

This scream wasn't one of outrage. It was one of terror. Clasping the gun tightly in his hand, he headed toward the house. He had to make sure nobody else got hurt because of what he'd done. Well, nobody but whoever was making his family scream in terror.

Chapter 15

Jake had recognized the house when the rental company had given him the GPS location of the SUV Lillian had stolen from him. Of course, he hadn't told them it was stolen, just that his girlfriend had taken off to run an errand and forgotten where she'd parked it. He hadn't wanted them to call the police. At least not yet.

He'd wanted to find out if she was trying to get away or trying to get that flash drive. But when he'd seen the house, Jake had known what she was after.

Donny had been dating Katie when Jake was dating Lillian. So he'd remembered her, just like Lillian must have. And while Lillian had been talking to her at the front door, Jake had snuck in the back, figuring Donny, the little weasel, was probably hiding in her bed.

When he'd found that empty, he'd moved to the other rooms—searching for Donny and for that flash drive. It was too bad he hadn't been quieter because he'd woken up the kids and scared the hell out of them.

He'd never been good with kids. Hopefully, the one Lillian was carrying wasn't his—for the kid's sake. For so many reasons...

"Shhh." He'd tried to quiet the kid. But it had lasted only moments before the mother burst into the room and screamed even louder than the kid had.

Then Lillian appeared behind her, her blue eyes wide with shock. "Jake!"

He needed to get her out of here. If a neighbor had heard all the screaming and called 911...

He stepped around Katie, who swung her fists at him, and he grasped Lillian's arm. "We need to get out of here before the police come."

"You better run!" Katie shouted at him. "Pervert!" She swung at him again and hit his shoulder as he headed toward the stairs.

He ushered Lillian down the steep steps of the old house. He kept his hand around her arm to steady her. She slipped once and nearly fell but he caught her. As they neared the open front door, shots rang out—chipping wood from the jamb.

Katie screamed again.

"Stay up there!" Jake shouted at her. "Get the kids to the back of the house!"

Katie disappeared from the top of the stairs, so hopefully, she had done as he'd told her. But Jake didn't wait to find out; he tugged Lillian toward the back of the house, careful to keep himself between her and the front door, where the shooter must have been standing. The shots continued to ring out, breaking the picture window, rustling the blinds, before plunging into the drywall over Jake's head.

Lillian froze, as if paralyzed with fear.

"Come on!" Jake yelled. Whatever patience he'd possessed—which had never been much—had left him when he'd awakened alone.

Lillian gasped at his shout but then she moved, running through the kitchen with him toward the back door. He stepped out first, with his gun drawn, but the shooter was still at the front of the house. Jake could have slipped around the front; he could have taken out the gunman.

But he had a feeling he knew who it was and Lillian wouldn't want him to kill her brother. He remembered how she'd screamed when she'd thought he might hurt her dad and her brother Dave. And if that was dimwit Donny with the gun, there was no talking to him now—not unless Jake shot him to make him stop shooting.

Then they would get no answers.

Lillian had parked the SUV down the block. Jake had seen it when the cab had dropped him off. So keeping low on the sidewalk behind the cars parked at the curb, he led her to the SUV. When they opened the doors, though, the gunman saw the lights flash on, and swung his weapon toward them.

One bullet glanced off the metal—another cracked the plastic of the side mirror.

"Keys!" Jake shouted.

And Lillian passed them over to him.

He jammed them in the ignition and started the SUV. The shots kept firing, even as he pulled away.

But this gunman was a worse marksman than the other guys who'd fired at them. They escaped with all the glass intact.

But Jake was not appeased. He was furious.

Lillian had never seen Jake like this. He was so angry that his face was flushed, and his pulse pounded in a jagged vein distended across his temple. Was he angry over getting shot at or over her sneaking out while he was sleeping?

The first question that she asked, though, was, "How did you find me?"

Did their minds work the same? After making love, had he come to the same conclusion she had?

"The rental has built-in GPS," he said, "for just these instances—when someone steals it."

"I didn't steal it!" She didn't need a charge of auto theft added to the embezzlement charge. "I borrowed it."

"You didn't ask permission."

"Because you would have said no," she replied.

"And with good reason!"

She'd had a good reason. "I was looking for Donny."

"I figured as much."

"You did?" She was nearly as shocked as she'd been when Timmy had screamed. "You didn't think I was on the run?" She had been worried that leaving like she had, after they'd made love, would make him think he'd been right—that she was just like her family, trying to elude justice. But she'd been trying to make sure it was served—to Tom Kuipers.

"That was my first thought," he admitted.

She glanced over at him. The streetlights passing over them illuminated his face through the windshield. His pulse was still pounding in that vein. "You're lying," she said. "That wasn't your *first* thought."

She knew what he'd thought—the same thing she would have if she was him. "You thought I used sex to trick you…"

His face flushed again. But it wasn't with anger now. "That might have crossed my mind, as well," he admitted.

And she didn't think that thought had completely left it. "That wasn't the case at all," she assured him. "I couldn't fall asleep—I just kept thinking about the flash drive and Donny. And it dawned on me that he might have gone back to an ex." Now her face flushed with embarrassment as she realized it might sound to Jake as if she'd made an assumption about the two of them.

She and Jake weren't back together. He hadn't come to her like Donny had come to Katie, begging for another chance. Jake had come for her—to take her into custody so he could collect another bounty for a Davies fugitive.

"Not that we're back together," she hurriedly added. "We're not. We can't be."

"Because you hate me," he murmured.

"I don't even know who you are now," she said, and she pulled the wad of papers from the glove box. "I don't know if you lied to me when we met, or if you're living the lie now as Jake Howard. Who are you really?"

He took the papers from her hand and tossed them

back into the glove box. "I'm trying to keep you safe," he said.

"By using aliases?" Which was the alias, though, and which was the real Jake?

"I'm making sure that nobody can track us down," he said. "But it's hard to keep you safe when you run off again and again."

"I didn't run off." This time. She couldn't argue that she had run away from him before, though. "I needed to find Donny. And I didn't think he'd talk to me if you were around."

He sighed. She took it as an acknowledgment that she was right. Donny wouldn't have talked with him present.

"He didn't talk," Jake agreed. "He just started shooting."

"No! That wasn't Donny shooting," she said. "One of us must have been followed from the hotel."

And now Jake pulled the SUV into the parking lot of that same hotel. "Why did you bring me back here? It's not safe. I just said one of us must have been followed from here."

He shook his head. "That was one gunman wildly firing those shots. And Kuipers hasn't ever sent just one man after us."

That was true. But what he was saying...

She shook her head. "Donny doesn't even own a gun."

"He does now," Jake said. "But lucky for us, he's a horrible shot."

Donny would be, since he had never fired one before. Lillian was the only grandchild that Gran had taught how to shoot. She hadn't wanted to be responsible for teaching the boys. She'd figured they'd learn on their own.

Lillian still couldn't accept that Donny had a gun, though. "My gran is the only one with a real gun. My dad and brothers only use airsoft ones." Her face heated with embarrassment because she knew Jake was well aware of what they had used those guns to do. Rob people.

Jake uttered a ragged sigh and pushed one of his hands through his overly long hair. "Those were real bullets, Lillian. Pellets wouldn't have made it through the wood and drywall."

And nearly into Jake's head. Those shots had come so close to hitting him. Lillian shuddered. But she still didn't want to believe it. "That wasn't him. He wouldn't shoot bullets into Katie's house."

Jake shrugged. "Maybe he heard her or the kid scream, and he thought…"

What Lillian had thought, that Jake was a bad man who'd broken into the house. Even after learning his identity—whatever that was—Donny would have still thought Jake was a bad man breaking into the house.

"I need to go back without you," she said. "I can get Donny to talk to me, to hand over that flash drive." If he still had it.

He hadn't given it to her lawyer like she'd requested. But he wouldn't have given it to Tom Kuipers, would he?

"They're gone," Jake said. "They probably took off the moment we did."

"You don't know that. Katie has kids. A house.

A job. She can't just take off," Lillian said. "She's there."

"And so are the police by now," Jake said. "If you go back, you'll be taken right into custody." He turned off the ignition and turned toward her. "But maybe that wouldn't be such a bad thing."

She gasped. How could he say that? After what they'd just shared?

Sex. That was all it was. At least for him.

For her, it had been so much more.

Another mistake. A terrible mistake. Because she was beginning to fall for him, even though she had no idea who he really was. Last time she'd done that, she'd been unaware. This time she had no excuse.

Seymour had actually considered going home tonight. At least to shower and maybe sleep in his bed instead of slumped over his desk. But when he headed toward the office door, someone started pounding on it. "Police, open up!"

He could have asked if they had a warrant. But it was late. And he didn't care. He opened the door. "Yes, Officer?"

The cop didn't look familiar to him. And Seymour knew most of River City PD's finest. He wasn't even sure if that was really a River City PD uniform. The color was right—the navy blue. But the insignia...

Didn't the shield on the shoulder look different? More like a Boy Scout badge than what real officers wore.

He quickly looked away from it, though. He would go along with the ruse. After that call that had threatened his life, it was safer than letting the guy know he was onto him.

"Seymour Tuttle?" the man asked. He was an older guy, probably in his fifties, but still younger than Seymour. He had hair, too, but it was mostly gray. And he had some kind of bearing about him that made Seymour think of Jake, like a military bearing or something.

Seymour nodded. "Yes, Officer…?"

He wanted a name. But the man didn't provide one.

Instead, he launched into a monologue. "We've been investigating several shootings around the city and outskirts of it the past two nights. We believe these incidents involve a fugitive and perhaps one of your bounty hunters."

Seymour shared the man's suspicions. But he just shrugged. "I don't know anything about that but what I've seen on the news."

Because Jake was damn well not talking to him, or when he did, he wasn't telling him the damn truth.

"You didn't post bond for a Lillian Davies?"

It was already a matter of public record—as his threatening caller had informed him, so Seymour nodded. "I did."

"And since she missed her court date, she is now in violation of her parole."

Seymour nodded again.

"So you've sent a bounty hunter to bring her back?"

He had sent several now, thanks to Jake not doing his job. Of course, the O'Hanigans had backed off, though, which had surprised Seymour. Usually they'd do anything to collect a bounty, especially if they could beat Jake to it.

This visit was another surprise, one that had a chill chasing down his spine. "Has there been another incident?" he asked.

Had something happened to Jake?

Again, the officer didn't answer his question. "We need to know the identity of the bounty hunter you've sent to apprehend Lillian Davies."

Seymour shrugged and lied, "I don't know who went after her. I post the fugitives, and every bounty hunter can go after them."

"I need a list of your bounty hunters, then," the officer said.

Seymour resisted the urge to smile. A beat cop in a uniform wouldn't have been sent to investigate a string of shootings. A detective would have been sent instead.

"You'll need to show me a warrant for that list," Seymour said.

The man showed his gun instead, pulling it from the holster to point it at Seymour. "Here's my warrant, old man."

Because sometimes fugitives came after him before he could go after them, Seymour had a panic switch on his key chain. He hit it now and alarms blared and lights flashed.

Over the commotion, he shouted, "The real police will be on their way soon."

So if the guy pulled that trigger, there was the possibility he would be seen fleeing the murder scene. That possibility must have occurred to the gray-haired man, as well, because instead of pulling that trigger, he turned and ran.

Through the door the guy had left open, Seymour

watched the pseudo-cop jump into the passenger's side of a white cargo van.

That hadn't been a prank call from one of Lillian Davies's idiot relatives that Seymour had received the other night. Whoever was after Lillian Davies didn't want her getting brought to the authorities.

They wanted her brought to the morgue and apparently they now wanted Jake brought along with her.

Chapter 16

For the first time since Jake had known Seymour Tuttle he heard fear in the old man's voice. From all the years he'd dealt with criminals, the bail bondsman had seen so much that nothing had ever seemed to faze him.

Until now.

"I don't like this, Jake," Tuttle told him through the cell phone speaker.

Jake didn't like it, either, any of it. "Did you get a plate for the van? And did you give that information to the police?"

"There was dirt smeared over the plate," Tuttle replied. "I couldn't read it."

These guys knew what they were doing, knew how to elude the police.

"Damn it."

"Jake, you need to talk to the police," Tuttle urged him. "The real police. You're getting in too deep."

He knew that. He felt like he had the last time he'd been seeing Lillian Davies, like he was going under and couldn't fight his way to the surface anymore.

But he admitted nothing to Tuttle, who added, "You're harboring a fugitive, Jake. That will land you in jail."

He couldn't argue that, either. He would undoubtedly be facing criminal charges himself before all this was over. He just hoped it ended with the charges against Lillian being dropped.

"So are the police going to investigate Tom Kuipers now?" Jake asked.

"Why?" Tuttle asked. "Nothing has been traced back to him. Not that call to my office. Not that van with the smeared plate."

"Not those men who died?" Jake asked.

"Nope," Tuttle replied. "There was no record of any connection between them."

Jake cursed again. Kuipers was good. Maybe too good to be caught. And if his guilt couldn't be proven, Lillian's innocence couldn't be, either.

"You need to bring her in," Tuttle said. "Or this isn't going to end well for either of you."

Jake clicked off the cell, not that he thought Tuttle would try tracing the call or anything. Seymour wouldn't turn him in to the police. The O'Hanigans probably wouldn't, either. But it would eventually be discovered that he was helping Lillian. And then he'd be in trouble.

"He's right," Lillian said from the bed across the hotel room. She was lying down yet, with her head resting on the pillow, but her beautiful blue eyes were open. "This isn't going to end well."

He'd had the call on speaker but with the volume turned low. He hadn't wanted to wake her. But he wondered now if she'd actually been sleeping.

She needed to rest. There were dark circles beneath her eyes, marring the silky perfection of her skin.

"Are you okay?" he asked. He'd brought her back food from a nearby diner. But the burger and fries probably hadn't been the healthiest meal for a pregnant woman.

She sighed, sat up and pushed her hair back from her face. The pale blond locks tangled around her shoulders. "No. I won't be okay until we find that damn flash drive. You should have let me go back and talk to Donny."

"And I told you Donny was already gone," he reminded her. "And the police were probably swarming the place after the reports of shots fired."

"Will you face charges, too?" she asked as she sat up, her face tight with concern. "For helping me?"

He nodded. "Yes, I was supposed to bring you in the moment I found you."

"Why didn't you?" she asked. "Do you feel that guilty for deceiving me?"

He had felt guilty for a long time. Now he wasn't sure what he felt...except protective. And not just of her.

"Is that baby mine?" he asked.

Her teeth sank into her bottom lip, and she hesitated a long moment before nodding.

"Damn it..."

She flinched. "I didn't plan on getting pregnant," she said. "It just happened."

"I know." That night they hadn't used protection. That wondrous night, like the night before.

He uttered a ragged sigh.

"Are you really that upset with me?"

"I'm upset you didn't tell me." Maybe if he'd known months ago, she wouldn't have been framed and arrested. If he'd been involved in her life, she might not have been in the danger she was.

Or she might have been in more. His job wasn't the safest career choice.

"I knew you wouldn't be happy," she said. "You probably wanted to forget about me as much as I wanted to forget about you."

He flinched now. But he deserved the emotional blow. And maybe he was a sucker for more, because he approached the bed and sat down beside her. Then he reached out and placed his hand over her burgeoning belly. The baby moved beneath his touch, fluttering and kicking, as if he was doing somersaults in her womb.

They had created a life together.

"Are you upset, then?" he asked. "Are you mad that you're pregnant?"

"No," she said—immediately and vehemently. "I am so happy about this baby. I can't wait to hold him. To love him."

But it was clear that she already loved him or her.

Her eyes shimmered with a sheen of tears, and her voice cracked with emotion when she added, "I just don't want to do that in jail."

"I don't want you to have this baby in jail, either," he said.

But he wasn't sure how the hell he was going to keep her out of it. Tom Kuipers had covered his tracks well. Right now, he had set himself up to look like the victim—instead of the bad man that he was. And Lillian had been made to look like the bad person: the criminal.

Maybe they should just run. It had worked for Jake's father. He had eluded capture for decades.

As the baby flipped in her stomach, Lillian's heart flipped in her chest. But that was over the look of awe on Jake's face. She wasn't the only one falling in love with their unborn baby. Jake loved the child, too. That was probably why he hadn't turned her over to the authorities yet.

He didn't want their baby born in jail any more than she did. As if to confirm her suspicion, he asked, "When are you due?"

"Four weeks," she replied. She imagined a clock ticking off the minutes as she raced to prove her innocence.

But she wasn't racing anymore. She had no idea where to look for Donny or that flash drive. She blinked back tears as she thought of her younger brother's betrayal.

Nobody had followed them back to the hotel. Jake had to be right. That had been her brother shooting at them.

"Why didn't Donny help me?" she asked. "What the hell did he do with that flash drive?"

"He probably sold it to Tom Kuipers," Jake said.

She bit back a curse, not certain what the baby could hear from inside her womb. No doubt he could feel her anxiety because he moved around even more.

And that look of awe and wonder crossed Jake's handsome face again.

"At least he'll have half your genes," she said. "Maybe he'll have a chance at a normal life." Even if he was born in jail…

The look of wonder left Jake's expression, replaced with one of dread.

"What's wrong?" she asked, alarmed that he looked so upset. She covered his hand with hers.

He shook his head, and he jerked his hand back from her belly and from her touch. He fisted it at his side, as if he wanted to hit something. Or someone…

She couldn't blame him if he wanted to hit Donny. She wanted to hit her younger brother, too. But she didn't think Donny had upset Jake this time. She had and she hadn't meant to. "Jake?"

"You asked about my two names," he said, and his voice sounded odd, almost hollow, as if he was entirely devoid of emotion.

She knew that wasn't true, though. She'd seen his fury. And she'd felt his passion. Jake wasn't hollow. He was deep and full of secrets and lies.

Was he about to reveal one of his secrets?

"Yes," she said, prodding him now. He had shut her down when she'd asked him earlier that evening about his two names, just as he had shut her down every other time she'd asked too personal of a question.

"Jacob Williams is my real name," he said. "Not Jake Howard."

"So you're a bounty hunter under an assumed

name?" she asked. "Did you do that to protect yourself from vengeful fugitives?"

It made sense. His was a dangerous profession. Not every fugitive he apprehended was armed with airsoft guns like her dad and brother Dave. Even Donny had bought a real weapon now.

She shivered as she thought of how close some of those bullets had come to hitting her and Jake. What the hell had her brother been thinking?

He had been protecting himself with no regard for her. Gran had warned her that all Davies men were selfish. Since that selfishness was all Lillian had known, she'd thought all men were like that. That was why she'd guarded her heart so well—until Jake, with his charm and generosity, had stolen it.

"I legally changed my name to Jake Howard years ago," he told her. "I didn't want the same name as my father anymore. So I took my mother's maiden name."

At last, he was talking about his family. Since she carried his baby, maybe he'd realized she had a right to know. Her baby carried half his DNA. She bit her bottom lip, so that she wouldn't ask him any questions. She didn't want to interrupt when he'd finally started talking.

"I figured it would be confusing, too," he said, "for a US marshal to have the same name as a wanted fugitive."

"What?" the question slipped out with her shock.

"My father is a fugitive," he said. "He's been on the run for two decades—ever since I was thirteen."

Her family had never managed to elude capture for more than a couple months. And then everything

she knew about Jake—everything that was Jake—
fell into place for her.

"That's why you became a US marshal," she said.
It wasn't a question now. It was a certainty. "You
wanted to catch your father?"

"You probably don't understand that," he said.
"Even after how they treat you, you have this sense
of loyalty to your family."

They had tested that loyalty lately—especially
Donny.

"I don't know the situation," she said. "So of
course I don't understand. What did he do, Jake?"
And she shivered at the look that crossed his face.

It was a look of horror now, as if he was reliving
whatever it was. As if he'd been there.

She shuddered now as she guessed—even before
he told her—what it was.

"He killed my mother."

Despite having guessed it, she gasped in shock.
Leaping up from the bed, she closed her arms around
him, holding him as his big body trembled in her
embrace.

And she realized why he'd never told her. It was
because it was too hard for him to talk about. It was
obviously too hard for him to take comfort, too, because he pulled away from her. "I grew up without
a mother," he said. "I don't want this baby to grow
up without one, too."

And that was why he'd been helping her. It wasn't
because he loved her—like she loved him. Despite
this realization, she couldn't fight how she felt any
longer. All the feelings she'd once had for him rushed
back even stronger.

She loved Jake Howard.

* * *

"This is the guy," the security chief said as he dropped a photo onto the table. "All of Tuttle's bounty hunters are licensed, so I searched through public records for copies of those licenses and recognized him."

Tom glanced down at the picture, and anger coursed through him. The guy, with his thick dark hair and chiseled face, was the kind of good-looking that it wouldn't matter if he was broke, he'd still get women.

Tom needed the money to get women. Lots of money.

"Who is he?"

"Jake Howard."

"I don't give a damn what his name is," Tom said. "Who is he?"

"A bounty hunter, just like you thought," Archie Wells confirmed.

But there was more and Tom waited for it.

"He's also an ex-marine and a former US marshal," Archie added, and it was obvious from the awe in his voice that the respect he'd already had for the guy had grown.

So Jake Howard was freaking Rambo.

Tom cursed. This was not good. "If he's a bounty hunter, why the hell hasn't he brought her to jail?"

"He has a history with her," the chief said.

Tom snorted.

Of course he did.

Women like Lillian Davies didn't go for guys like Tom, despite the money. But they would go for a guy who looked like this.

Tom hadn't even bothered to make a pass at the little accountant, though, because when he'd hired her, it had been with the intention of setting her up to take the blame for stealing the money he'd been planning to steal. He'd been well aware of her family's reputation, so he hadn't figured anyone would believe she was innocent.

But apparently this Jake Howard believed she was. He'd risked his life for her.

Wells continued, "He brings in all her family members for jumping bail. He must have gotten to know her through that."

"We need to track him down," Tom said. Maybe that would be easier than tracking down Lillian Davies, since his guys had failed dismally at that.

But it wasn't just Lillian that Tom wanted. He wanted that damn flash drive, too. He'd paid for it. It was his.

If it even existed...

Chapter 17

The bars slid closed behind Jake, locking him in with the criminals he'd brought here. To jail.

Hell, this wasn't jail. It was prison. But because they weren't violent criminals, like his missing father, it was minimum security. There was no glass between him and Dave and Donald Davies Senior. He walked across the room to where they waited at a round metal table for him. With benches around it, it looked like some kind of picnic table at a park. But there were bars instead of trees surrounding them.

"I'm surprised you agreed to see me," he said.

"You said it's about Lillian," her father said. And despite his criminal ways, maybe he did care about his only daughter.

"She's in trouble," Jake said.

"What? You knock her up?" Dave asked with a snort of amusement.

They didn't know she was pregnant. Of course, she'd been gone for six months, waiting for trial. By her own account, that was the last time she had seen Donny in person—when she'd given him that flash drive.

And she'd said that she hadn't visited her dad and oldest brother since he'd apprehended them. They were still refusing to talk to her.

So why had they agreed to talk to him?

Apparently, it was curiosity, because her dad asked, "Why are you here, Howard? Do you want *us* to help you apprehend *her*?"

Maybe that was good, that they didn't know she was already with him, waiting in the leased SUV down the street from the prison. Outside of camera range.

Hopefully, she was staying in the back seat, like he'd told her, where the windows were tinted and no one could see inside. He hated being away from her... except for last night.

Last night he'd stayed outside the hotel room. He'd given her the excuse that he needed to stand guard while she slept. But that hadn't been the case at all.

After he'd told her about his family, he'd needed space. Because if he'd taken the comfort she'd offered him, he would have lost control. With his emotions as raw as bringing up the past made them, he wouldn't have been able to show her the gentleness she and their baby deserved.

His baby...

The child was his. She'd confirmed it. But even before she had, he'd known. He'd felt the connection.

It was as strong as the one he had with the baby's mother.

"Howard!" Don Senior said, snapping his fingers in his face. "What the hell's wrong with you?"

He was desperate. That was his only reason for seeking out these two degenerates. "You need to talk to your son."

Don glanced over at Dave. "We talk all the time."

They were probably cell mates. They looked more like brothers than father and son. They were both short and skinny with tattoos and greasy black hair and small dark eyes. They looked nothing like Lillian with her pale hair and blue eyes. She must have looked like her mother.

"You need to talk to your youngest son," Jake clarified. "He has a flash drive with files on it that Lillian downloaded to prove her innocence, and he hasn't turned it over to the authorities like she asked him to do for her."

Dave snorted again. "And why the hell would *we* help *her* after she helped you get us in here?"

"She didn't help me," Jake said. "She had no idea I was a bounty hunter."

Dave snorted again. "Bounty hunter. You're public enemy number one to every member of the Davies family. There's no way she couldn't have known who the hell you are. We've been talking about you for years."

But there was a way she hadn't known—because he'd lied to her and Lillian was entirely too trusting.

Jake ignored Dave and focused on her father, appealing to the man's paternal instincts—instincts Jake had already developed himself for that baby she was carrying. "She's not just in danger of going to jail," he told Donny Senior. "Someone's trying to *kill* her."

The older man stared at him for several long moments, as if trying to gauge Jake's truthfulness. Then he shrugged off whatever concern he should have been feeling, and he stood up to leave.

"You're not going to help her?" Jake asked, both shocked and outraged. But he, better than most, should have known you couldn't trust family.

Don Senior shook his head and said, "She's already dead to us."

Lillian must have fallen asleep in the back seat because she jerked awake as the SUV started moving. Fear rushed through her as she worried that it wasn't Jake driving. But then she sat up and identified the driver's head as the back of Jake's, his dark hair falling over the collar of his black shirt.

She released a shuddery breath of relief and tried to meet his gaze in the rearview mirror. But he looked away from her. Maybe he was just focusing on the road. Or maybe he still felt awkward about what he'd revealed last night.

Ever since his admission, he'd been distant.

She couldn't imagine the horror of his childhood. It was clear from his expression when he'd told her what his father had done that, while it had shocked Lillian, it hadn't been a surprise to him. His father must have abused his mother for years. And Jake, as their child, would have witnessed all that.

Her heart ached for everything he had endured and for everything he had lost. Despite his distance now, Lillian felt closer to him than she ever had. She understood him so much more than she had before.

He was focused on apprehending fugitives because of his father eluding justice. He didn't want anyone else getting away with their crimes.

What about her? Did he really believe her?

He must or, surely, he would have brought her to jail by now. For one horrifying moment, she'd thought he'd intended to turn her in when he'd driven up to the prison. But then he'd told her his plan to appeal to her dad and brother to help her with Donny.

They'd come out of hiding before to protect her. He'd thought they might come to her aid again.

"What did they say?" she asked. But she wasn't as hopeful as he'd been.

His gaze met hers briefly in the rearview mirror before he quickly looked away again. And she knew…

It hadn't been good.

"What did they say?" she asked again. "Did they agree to reach out to Donny?"

He shook his head, and his dark hair swept across his collar. "No."

Just like his admission regarding his past, even though she'd suspected the truth before he'd shared it with her, she gasped with shock. "They won't?"

Her own family had refused to help her.

"No," he said. "They refused to talk to me at all."

Jake was not a good liar. Maybe that was why he'd given her his real name all those months ago. It was obviously easier for him to tell the truth than lie.

But this time she appreciated that he wasn't telling her the truth. She knew it would only hurt her.

Her family hadn't forgiven her for being involved with Jake.

What would they say if they knew she loved the bounty hunter?

Probably nothing at all. They had refused to talk to her months ago. All but for Donny…

And now she couldn't reach out to him, either. She slid her hands over her belly. Her baby was the only family she had now.

Donny dropped into the chair across the metal table from his dad and brother. Sweat trickled down between his shoulder blades. He hated this place and had vowed, like Lillian had, that he would never wind up here.

Prison.

But they'd summoned him with a phone call to his brother Dylan. After last night, he'd been staying there since Katie had thrown him out.

She wanted nothing to do with him again. And he couldn't blame her. He'd shot up her house.

Of course, he'd been trying to hit the intruder. Not her or the kids or Lillian.

But his hand was still shaking from how close he had come to shooting her. He'd had no business buying that gun. "Why'd you guys want to see me?"

He'd told them about the flash drive when Lillian had given it to him six months ago. Instead of just doing what she'd asked of him, like he should have, he'd asked their opinion about what to do with it. Now he wished like hell he'd never taken their advice.

"Jake Howard came to see us," Dave said with a snort of disgust. He hated the bounty hunter.

They all did.

But for Lillian.

Katie had told Donny that his sister was pregnant. Why the hell hadn't Lillian told him that? But maybe she hadn't known six months ago when she'd given him that flash drive.

"What did Jake want?" Donny asked. But he knew. Jake was with Lillian, but he hadn't brought her to jail yet. Maybe he cared about her, too.

"He wants you to give that flash drive to the police," his father said.

Donny wanted nothing to do with the police, but he admitted, "I should give it back to Lillian." Then she could use it however she wanted.

"You should ask that boss of hers for more money," Dave said.

Donny had already burned through everything Tom Kuipers had paid him—for an empty flash drive. Good thing he'd done the drop through an exchange at a bus locker. Donny had taken out the money and left the blank flash drive. And he'd slipped away before any of Kuipers's men had had a chance to grab him. But he'd seen them there. That was why he'd had Katie stage a disturbance, screaming that one of the men had tried to assault her.

Donny had barely escaped that time. He wasn't sure he would be so lucky if he tried to scam Tom Kuipers again.

"What about Lillian?" he asked. "Her boss is a maniac. He's trying to kill her."

The color drained from their father's face. They'd

pulled off some scams and thefts, but they'd never really hurt anyone. Nor had they ever really been hurt, like Tom Kuipers wanted to hurt Lillian.

"She has Jake Howard to take care of her," Dave bitterly replied.

"She's not the only one in danger," Donny said. And he wasn't talking about himself.

Kuipers had no idea he had that flash drive. At least Donny didn't think so. Of course, one of those shootings had been near his apartment building, so maybe Kuipers had figured it out. Donny hadn't told his family about that shooting, though, so they didn't realize he could be in danger, too.

"Who the hell cares that Jake Howard is in danger, too?" Dave asked. He was letting his hatred of the bounty hunter blind him to whatever love he had yet for Lillian.

How could he forget that she was their sister? Their only sister? And so much like Mom...

It felt like someone was squeezing Donny's heart as he thought of their sweet mother. She would be so disappointed in him.

"I'm not talking about Howard," he said. He didn't care about the bounty hunter, although he was glad he hadn't hit him last night. He wouldn't have wanted to kill the father of his sister's baby. His niece or nephew.

"She's pregnant," Donny said.

His father gasped now. And Donny remembered how old the old man was, even though he didn't look his age at all. He looked closer to thirty-five, like Dave was. But then Dave looked older than thirty-five now. Prison had probably aged both of them.

Dad was too old for these kinds of shocks. So wouldn't it kill him if someone killed Lillian? Because Tom Kuipers seemed pretty damn determined to make sure that she didn't just end up in jail.

He wanted her in the morgue.

Chapter 18

Jake had called in a favor from a friend who was still with the US Marshals. He'd found a better place to take Lillian than a hotel that took cash. But he wouldn't have access to the place for very long.

The guy only owed him so big a favor.

Time was running out.

Obviously, there weren't any warrants out for his arrest yet, or Jake would have been taken into custody at the prison when they'd run his name through the system. As he'd thought, Tuttle and the O'Hanigans hadn't admitted to anyone that Jake already had Lillian Davies in his custody.

They were protecting him. He wasn't surprised that Tuttle would. He knew Jake worked harder to protect his money than any other bounty hunter did. But why hadn't the O'Hanigans turned him in?

Sure, the rivalry had been more on their side than Jake's and no doubt encouraged by Tuttle, but he'd hit Shane over the head. They really owed him one for that. But they must not have said anything yet.

But what about her family?

Would one of them turn him in?

He wouldn't put anything past the Davies family.

"Are you okay?" Jake asked when Lillian stepped out of the bathroom.

She had showered and put on one of the outfits he'd bought her. She looked beautiful in the blue dress she wore. She hadn't needed the makeup she'd asked him to buy for her, but she'd used it to hide the dark circles he knew she still had. It didn't hide the redness of her eyes or her swollen lids, though.

She'd been crying.

"I'm sorry," he said.

"Why?" she asked.

"It's my fault."

Her lips curved into a slight smile. "And here I thought Mr. Kuipers stole the money."

That was her defense—humor. It was how she'd dealt with what must have been a tough life. She kept an upbeat attitude. But it had to be a struggle for her to manage that now—with men trying to kill her and her own family turning against her.

"This rift with your family," he said, as guilt twisted his guts. "It's my fault."

"You were only doing your job," she said. "I was never mad that you brought them to jail."

She was only mad that he'd used her to do it.

"I'm sorry," he said again, hating that he'd hurt her then. And now...

Going to her family today had been a bad idea. But he'd run out of good ones.

"I have my friend with the US Marshals investigating Kuipers," he said. But the guy hadn't made any promises about when he could manage to look into it. He had several more pressing cases.

She shrugged as if it didn't matter. Maybe she'd given up hope. And maybe Jake should stop trying to bolster her hopes. But he needed that hope himself.

"We'll figure out how to prove your innocence," he said. And he pulled her trembling body into his arms.

She laid her head on his chest and clutched his shirt in her hands. Her tears dampened the material over his heart, which hurt with her fear and pain.

He stroked his hands down her back. But he had no idea how to comfort her.

Then she eased back and stared up into his face. And he knew...

He lowered his head to hers and kissed her. As always, just that whisper-soft brush of lips across lips ignited the passion between them.

Her face flushed with it.

His pulse raced with it.

"Lillian..."

Lillian needed Jake in a way she had never needed anyone else. She didn't need him just to protect her. Or to help her prove her innocence. She needed him to breathe, for her heart to beat.

And she knew that was crazy. He was only helping her because of the baby. Their baby...

But she pushed that thought from her mind. Then

when he swung her up in his arms, every thought left her mind. She could only feel—the passion, the need. She wrapped her arms around his shoulders, clinging to him as he carried her into the bedroom.

Instead of laying her on the bed, he set her on her feet, her body sliding down the length of his. She felt his erection straining behind the fly of his jeans.

He wanted her.

She was pregnant and huge. How the hell did he still find her sexy?

But the way he looked at her, his eyes dark with desire made her feel sexy.

"You look so beautiful," he said. He skimmed his fingers over her shoulder, over the dress he'd bought her.

She loved it, too. He'd done so well choosing clothes for her, while she'd hidden in the SUV in the mall parking lot. Jake had been worried that someone might recognize her, if the police posted her photo as a wanted fugitive, so she hadn't been able to go into the store with him.

She hadn't needed to, though. He knew her taste better than she'd realized. He knew her.

"I almost hate to take this off you," he said. But yet, there was no hesitation when he bent down and lifted it from the hem and pulled it over her head.

Her hair tangled around her face before dropping over her bare shoulders. She wore her bra beneath the dress and a pair of panties that started below her belly.

Her big belly...

But instead of it turning Jake off, he leaned over and skimmed his lips over it. And his fingers shook a little as he ran them over the swollen mound.

"You are so beautiful," he said again as he straightened up.

She smiled, moved that he was so affected by her pregnancy.

Then he unclasped her bra and touched her breasts, sliding his thumbs over her nipples until they tightened. Pleasure shot through her, and a moan slipped from between her lips.

Jake groaned. Then he lowered his head and moved his mouth over her breasts. When his lips closed over one of her nipples, she cried out.

And he pulled back. "Did I hurt you?"

She shook her head. But the tension inside her was so intense it was almost painful. She needed the release only he could give her.

She needed him.

She reached for the button of his jeans, quickly undoing it before pulling down the tab of his zipper. Then she reached through the flap of his boxers and freed him.

His skin was smooth in her hand and pulsating with the same need for release that burned inside her.

"Lillian…" Her name sounded almost like a growl as Jake uttered it between clenched teeth. A muscle twitched in his cheek. "You're driving me crazy."

She continued to slide her hand up and down the length of him. And he groaned again. Then he dragged off his shirt and kicked off his jeans and boxers. When Lillian dropped to her knees, he lifted her up before she could close her mouth around his erection.

"You've tortured me enough," he told her. Then he laid her on the bed and he proceeded to torture her.

First, he focused all his attention on her breasts, lapping at the nipples, teasing and tugging on them.

She shifted on the bed as her pulse pounded in her core, demanding release.

Then he moved lower over the mound of her belly. He pulled off her panties and made love to her with his mouth until she arched off the bed and screamed his name.

The orgasm was intense, but it still wasn't enough. She needed him—inside her—as if he was part of her. And she part of him.

He must have needed to feel the same way because he moved onto the bed. Instead of lying on his back, he knelt on the mattress. Then he lifted her until she straddled his lap.

She reached between them, guiding his pulsing erection into her core. Biting her lip, she tried to hold in the cry of pleasure as she slid over him. But it slipped free.

Then his mouth moved over hers, and he nibbled on her lower lip before sliding his tongue into her mouth. He moved his hips, thrusting them up. But he stilled and sweat beaded on his brow. "I don't want to hurt you."

"You're not hurting me or the baby," she assured him. And she locked her arms around his shoulders and moved, sliding up and down the length of his erection.

He groaned again, sounding as if he was tortured. Maybe she was torturing him. And herself.

He moved with her. And finally, she found her release, crying out as she came. He tensed, then shuddered as he filled her.

She wanted to cry out again. She wanted to profess her love. But it wouldn't be fair to make that declaration now—not when she was so uncertain of her future.

Uncertain if she even had one…

And even if the charges were dropped against her, she wasn't sure Jake wanted to be back with her. If he had, he would have sought her out months ago. Wouldn't he?

While he was protecting her and he seemed to care about the baby they'd made, she wasn't sure that he cared about her—that he loved her like she loved him.

And she didn't want to wind up like her mother, dying of a broken heart. So she needed to keep the declaration and her feelings to herself.

Jake Howard had already hurt her once.

She couldn't let him—or anyone else—hurt her again.

Tom's cell rang but the caller ID came up blank. Whoever was calling didn't want his or her identity known. That was fine with Tom. If someone had finally killed Jake Howard and Lillian Davies, he didn't want their deaths linked to him.

There couldn't be any traceable record of calls between the killer and himself.

But disappointment tugged at him. He wanted to kill Lillian himself—right after he made damn sure that flash drive didn't exist.

He clicked the accept button. "Yes?"

"Mr. Kuipers?"

He recognized that voice, the one of the man

who'd swindled him. And despite the con artist's efforts to hide his identity, Tom had recently learned it. Archie Wells had a friend in security at the bus terminal, and he had managed to get the footage from the day Tom had been tricked into paying for a blank flash drive.

"Donny Davies," he said, letting the man know he was no longer anonymous.

Tom had his name and his death warrant signed.

There was a long pause.

"Nothing to say for yourself?" Tom asked.

"I don't have to talk," Donny said as he began to do just that. "All I have to do is turn over this flash drive to the authorities."

"If you were going to do that, you would have already," Tom said, which made him more certain that the thing had never existed.

Lillian Davies wasn't smart enough or brave enough to go after him. Was she?

"It will go to them if anything happens to me or my sister," Donny said.

Tom had played poker for years. He recognized a bluff when he heard one. "I don't believe you," he said. "If there was any evidence on that flash drive, your sister would not be a fugitive. She would have showed up in court with it in her hand."

And Tom would be the fugitive. At least he had the money and the means to elude justice, though.

Lillian Davies did not.

Even if she'd been in on the con with her brother, they hadn't asked for much money. They'd probably already burned through what Tom had had delivered to the locker in that bus terminal. And that must have been the real reason for this call: money.

"I have the flash drive," Donny said. "She doesn't. I can give it to her, though. Or I can give it to you."

Tom almost felt sorry for Lillian. Her own family was using her. All she had was that damn bounty hunter in her corner. But that wouldn't be for much longer.

Tom had put out a hit on Jake Howard, as well as her and her dim-witted brother. Because Donny Davies was such a dimwit, he would probably walk right into Tom's trap.

"I'll pay you," Tom said, "but I want to check out the flash drive before I give you another dime."

And once he'd checked it out, he would put a bullet in Donny Davies's pea brain.

Chapter 19

"You hit me over the head and expect me to do you a favor?" Shane O'Hanigan asked, his deep voice booming out of Jake's cell phone.

"Who said I hit you over the head?" Jake asked. One of Shane's brothers might have seen him do it, though.

But Shane hesitated long enough that Jake knew the guy had no proof. Just like he had no proof.

What the hell had Lillian's brother done with that flash drive? He needed help finding it and help finding Donny.

But Jake had learned a painful lesson when he'd deceived Lillian. Nothing good ever came of lying. And yet, getting close to Lillian—making that baby with her—hadn't been bad. The pain he'd caused her, though, was greater than what he'd caused Shane O'Hanigan.

"I did hit you," Jake admitted. "And I'm sorry."

Shane cursed him out for a long moment.

"It's not like I could actually hurt you, though," Jake said. "You're legendary for having a hard head." He was actually surprised he'd knocked the thick-headed Irishman unconscious. He must have hit him harder than he'd even intended. Guilt weighing on him, he asked, "Are you okay?"

Shane snorted. "You want to know if I'm well enough to do this favor you want me to do?"

"I need your help," Jake said, and it killed him to admit it.

Shane knew him well enough that he must have realized how hard that admission was for Jake to make, because he expelled a ragged breath that rattled the phone. "Wow, this is serious. So it is your kid she's carrying?"

"Yes."

"Congratulations?" Shane asked, clearly uncertain if this was news that would make Jake happy.

And with that question, Jake realized that he was happy. For himself. The poor kid was probably doomed. But Jake was happy that he would always have this connection with Lillian. That something good had come of the lies he'd told her.

"Thanks," Jake said. "I have to make sure the kid's not born in jail, though."

"That would suck," Shane agreed. "So what do you want our help with?"

"I need you to find Lillian's younger brother, Donny Davies."

"You're the expert on the Davies family." Shane snorted. "Obviously. So why do you think we can?"

"Because you're good," Jake begrudgingly admitted. They'd found his secret safe house, so he could no longer say that his rivals didn't have skills. He was counting on those skills to do what he couldn't.

"There's no bounty on him," Shane said.

"I'll pay you," he offered. He knew the brothers were like Tuttle—all about the money.

There was a long silence as if Shane was debating. Maybe he'd even muted the call to talk to his brothers. The O'Hanigans worked as a team. Jake envied them that, envied their genuine loyalty for each other despite their incessant bickering.

Finally, Shane spoke again. "I don't want your money, Jake."

He cursed. Damn it. He couldn't keep Lillian safe and track down her idiot brother.

But then Shane continued, "I want your car."

"What?"

"The Nova," Shane said. "I want that."

Jake nearly chuckled. Shane must not have seen the Nova in its current battered condition. "Man, you're driving a tough bargain."

"I'd rather drive that car," Shane said. "Is it a deal?"

Jake paused a long moment before adding, "On one condition."

"We're not going to kill him for you," Shane said.

A twinge of disappointment flashed through Jake. He'd have liked to kill Donny Davies Junior himself for all the trouble he'd caused Lillian.

"There's not even a bounty on him," Shane continued as if he might have considered it if there was.

"I don't want him dead," Jake said—because that would hurt Lillian. No matter how badly her family treated her, she still loved the selfish idiots. "I do want something he has, though. A flash drive that belongs to his sister."

"If I get this flash drive for you, you'll give me the car?" Shane asked.

Jake sighed. The classic vehicle was in rough shape now, but it had once been a beauty. He didn't have time to fix it any time soon, though. Hell, he might wind up in jail himself for helping Lillian. "Yeah, it's yours, then."

Shane clicked off the cell. And Jake felt a rush of hope. Maybe the O'Hanigans would be able to find Donny and that flash drive.

"You love that car," Lillian said from where she leaned against the doorjamb to the bedroom. Her hair was tousled around her face. And for once the dark circles were gone. She looked rested but worried, with a furrow on her brow.

He had loved that car, but he loved something else more. He shrugged. "I'm not holding my breath that they'll find him."

He didn't want her to hold her breath. That was why he said that, even though he was hopeful. He didn't want to build up her hopes only to have them dashed again. "They haven't ever been able to find any of the rest of your family."

But they had found Jake at his safe house. So the O'Hanigans were getting better. Or maybe the Davieses were getting better at being fugitives.

That might not be a bad thing, though, because if that flash drive wasn't found, Lillian would have to remain a fugitive.

There was no way she was having his baby in jail.

* * *

Lillian didn't want to live her life on the run—like most of her family. Like Jake's dad.

She wanted a real life with Jake and their baby. But she didn't hold out any more hope for that than she did for the other bounty hunters to find her brother and the flash drive. Even if this nightmare of her false arrest ended, she doubted Jake was willing to settle down.

If he'd really cared about her, he wouldn't have given up on them eight months ago. He would have fought for their relationship. He would have kept apologizing until he'd convinced her to forgive him.

She hadn't quite done that yet, though. She loved him. But she couldn't entirely get over how he'd used her.

"You won't have this baby in jail," Jake said, his voice deep with resolve.

But she wondered who he was trying to convince—her or himself?

She certainly wasn't convinced. "We can't count on finding that flash drive," she said.

If Donny had offered it to Mr. Kuipers for money, Tom wouldn't have paid out until he was certain he'd had it. And the minute he'd had it, he would have destroyed it.

That was probably why Donny had been avoiding Lillian. He didn't want to tell her what he'd done with it and that it was gone forever.

"So what are you saying?" Jake asked. "That you want me to let you get away? And you'll have this baby on the run?"

"You would let me get away?" she asked, and she felt a twinge of pain in her heart. He'd already done that once, so she shouldn't have been surprised. But now she was pregnant with his baby. Didn't that mean anything to him? Didn't she? Didn't their son or daughter?

She blinked against the sting of tears and cleared her eyes before meeting his gaze.

He'd hesitated a long moment—as if he was torn. Then he replied, "I should have brought you in the minute I found you in my truck back at the beach."

"You probably should have," she agreed. Because now he was in trouble, too.

"But I couldn't."

She was grateful for that, but Jake hadn't answered her question yet. He hadn't said whether or not he would let her go now.

But she didn't want it to come to that. She didn't want to keep running. "I have another idea."

He narrowed his dark eyes and stared at her with apparent suspicion. "Why do I feel as though I am not going to like this?"

Because he probably wouldn't. She didn't like it, either, but she didn't see any other way.

"I think I should meet with Mr. Kuipers," she said.

"You want to meet with the man who has been trying to kill you?" Jake asked, his voice cracking with outrage. "No way."

"It's the only way now." That the flash drive was gone. "I need to get him on record saying that he framed me."

Jake snorted. "And you think he's just going to admit that?"

"No," she said. "But I think I can get him talking."

Tom Kuipers was a notorious womanizer. In fact, she was the only female in the office he hadn't hit on and that had been before she was pregnant. If he hadn't found her attractive then, he certainly wouldn't now with as big as she was. So she wouldn't be able to charm him into talking. She would have to goad him into it.

Jake shook his head. "Absolutely not. It's too dangerous."

"So is going to prison," she said. Lillian knew herself—she wasn't strong enough to survive behind bars.

"We'll make sure it won't come to that."

"Don't make promises you can't keep, Jake," she warned him. At least he hadn't done that the last time. While he'd deceived her about who he was, he hadn't made her any promises.

"Lillian."

"You can put a wire on me or something," she said. "You must have done that when you were with the US Marshals."

"I have, but I won't now," he said. "Not for you."

She flinched. "Jake."

"It's too dangerous," he insisted.

But Lillian was beginning to believe it was the only way. And if Jake wouldn't help her, she would figure out how to pull it off on her own. She couldn't count on her family or on that flash drive turning up.

And Jake had proven eight months ago that she couldn't count on him.

She could only count on herself now.

Seymour slammed his fist against his desk. "Damn Jake Howard!"

Shane O'Hanigan just shrugged. He'd been standing in Tuttle's office when he'd taken that call from Jake—the one asking the O'Hanigans to find Donny Davies.

"That's not the Davies that Jake needs to be worried about apprehending," Seymour continued.

"We both know he already has the one you're talking about," Shane said.

And that was why Seymour was worried.

"There's no bounty on Donny," he continued. And he had finally learned his lesson now. If the guy got arrested, he was going to have to call another bail bondsman to get him out. Seymour wanted nothing to do with any of the damn Davies family ever again.

"There is a bounty on him now," Shane said with a devilish grin. "A 1969 Chevrolet Nova." He turned for the door, but before he could grasp the knob and pull it open, Seymour shouted for him to stop.

"You can't help him with this!"

"I don't really think it's helping him," Shane pointed out. "Not when he loses that sweet ride of his."

Jake wasn't going to need a car where he was going, either. If he didn't turn in Lillian Davies soon, there would be a warrant issued for him aiding and abetting a fugitive.

"He's in too deep," Seymour said.

Shane shrugged again. "It's his funeral."

That was exactly what Seymour was afraid of—not that Jake was going to wind up in jail but that he was going to wind up dead.

Chapter 20

The waiting was killing him. Jake wanted to be out looking for Donny himself. He wanted to personally shake that flash drive off of him. But he couldn't leave Lillian alone and unprotected, and he couldn't take her out again. Nearly every time he had, they'd been shot at.

They were lucky every bullet had missed. But eventually that luck was going to run out. That was why he'd refused to go along with her dangerous plan.

He'd seen the disappointment on her beautiful face. But it was gone now. She was smiling as she puttered around the kitchen. She was cooking.

She'd cooked for him a lot when they'd been going out eight months ago. Hell, they'd cooked together. But every time he'd tried to step into the kitchen this afternoon, she had shooed him out.

He couldn't help but wonder if she was preparing what she thought would be her last supper. "Do you have everything you need?" he asked.

The US Marshals used this safe house enough that the kitchen was pretty well stocked. Jake had only had to stop and pick up perishables before he'd brought Lillian here.

She glanced up at him from where she stirred something on the stove. "I could use a few more things," she said. But then she looked away again, as if unable to meet his gaze.

He studied her face. Her skin was flushed, maybe just from the heat of the stove and the oven. Or maybe for another reason.

Jake felt a chill of apprehension chase down his spine, just like he had when they'd pulled up at Donny's apartment that night. "You understand, right, that your plan is too dangerous?"

"I know it's dangerous," she said.

"Tom Kuipers is dangerous," he said. "You can't go anywhere near him."

She gestured around the small kitchen. "I don't see him here."

But Jake was afraid that if he left her alone—even for a minute—that she might either invite the guy over or offer to meet him somewhere.

He stepped into the kitchen with her. "I think you've done well with the ingredients you have." He leaned over her at the stove and kissed the side of her neck. She'd pulled her hair up into a ponytail.

She shivered now.

"Smells good," he said.

"It would be better with fresh ingredients," she said as she stirred what looked like pasta sauce.

"I wasn't talking about dinner," he said. And he brushed his lips along her neck.

Maybe he could make her forget all about her dangerous plan. Maybe he could make himself forget all about the frustration of waiting for the O'Hanigans to find Donny and that damn flash drive.

Maybe he could ease another kind of frustration… with her. He reached around her and turned off the stove. Then he swung her up in his arms.

She giggled and offered a weak protest, "Jake…"

"Dinner will keep," he said. "I'm hungry for something else now."

He was hungry for her. And for the past eight months, he'd had to fast. Now he couldn't get enough of her. He was careful to rein in his passion, though. He was gentle with her—as he undressed her, as he made love to her.

She moaned and arched, so responsive, so passionate.

Her breasts were so full, so round, so perfect.

He spent time caressing them, stroking his fingers over them, before he teased the nipples into tight buds. Then he closed his lips over one of those and gently tugged.

She arched off the bed and cried out. "Jake…"

She reached for him, but he clasped her wrists in one hand and held her off. He wanted to focus on her—on giving her pleasure.

But no matter how much pleasure he gave her, he didn't know if it could replace the pain he'd also given her eight months ago. He hadn't meant to hurt her then, though.

He hadn't meant to fall for her, either. But he hadn't been able to help himself.

He wanted to show her how much she meant to him. That was why he couldn't let her risk her life, not even for her freedom.

He moved his mouth lower, over her belly. Then he made love to her with his lips and his tongue.

She cried out again, louder. And she tugged her wrists free of his grasp. Then she dragged off his clothes and drove him out of his mind with her lips and her touch.

Finally, he rolled onto his back and pulled her on top of him. She slid down the length of him, her inner muscles clutching at him. And he felt like he was home—inside her. Like this was where he belonged.

He'd never felt like that before—except for eight months ago when he'd been with her. He'd been so shocked by how perfectly they'd felt together.

Jake had lost her once, and he didn't want to lose her again. But on some level, he felt like this might be the last time they would be together. So he drew out the tension, pulling out just when her muscles started to clutch him.

He drove them both out of their minds until they finally came together. She screamed. And he shouted as the pleasure overwhelmed him.

When they finally stopped panting for breath, Jake wrapped his arms around her, keeping her close to his side—where he was beginning to believe she belonged. And he fell asleep, imagining that she would always be there.

* * *

Once Jake had fallen asleep, Lillian forced herself to slip out of his arms and out of the bed. She hurried back toward the kitchen.

Jake had shut off the stove. Nothing was going to burn. But she wasn't worried about the food burning. She was worried about how she was going to slip Jake the sleeping pills she'd found in the bathroom cabinet.

The US Marshals must have planned for everything—even witnesses who were too anxious to sleep—because they provided some pretty powerful sleeping aids.

She wasn't sure how many to give Jake, though. He was so big. And she needed him asleep. Or he would never let her leave. He would never let her risk her life and their baby's.

Was she being too reckless?

No. She had to do this. It was the only way to prove her innocence. The only way she could be free to raise her baby and...

Love Jake. She already loved him. She didn't need to be free to do that.

Once she'd set the pot on the stove to simmer again, she reached for her phone. She'd had it turned off since the last time she'd tried calling Donny but had charged it.

She didn't bother trying to call Donny now.

Her brother had proven himself unworthy of her trust. Just as she would prove herself unworthy of Jake's when she sneaked out on him again. But hopefully, he would understand that she'd had to do it.

She had no choice.

And she was doing this as much for their child as for herself. So she scrolled through her contacts until she found another number, and she called it.

She called *him*.

"Hello?" he tentatively answered.

She had never called him before, so he probably didn't have her number in his contacts. She'd found his that night she'd broken in to the office and downloaded all those files to the flash drive.

"Mr. Kuipers?"

He released a breath that rattled in the phone. "Lillian Davies…" Then he chuckled and asked, "What can I help you with?"

"You can stop trying to kill me," she said, letting her anger and resentment slip into her voice. He was such a monster. It was bad enough that he'd framed her for his crime; now he wanted her dead, too.

But he acted all innocent when he replied, "Now, why would I be trying to do something like that?"

"So I don't turn over that flash drive to the authorities and prove that you framed me for your embezzling from your wife and father-in-law's company."

He snorted. "So that's your defense? No wonder you didn't show up for your trial. You're going to lose with wild accusations like that."

"I have the proof," she said.

Or she'd had it. How could she have been so naive as to trust Donny with it? Sure, he was her brother, but he was also their father's son.

Tom Kuipers chuckled again. "I find that quite hard to believe, Ms. Davies, or I doubt you'd have jumped bail like you have."

"I have it," she said. "But I figured it might be worth even more to you than it is to me."

"You want me to buy it?" He laughed again.

She named a price that was a lot of money to her but probably very little to him.

"That's steep," he said.

"It's nothing to you," she said. "I have the records that show exactly how much you stole and where you stashed it."

He sucked in a breath as if she'd punched him.

And she had hit him where it hurt—for him—in his wallet. She intended to hit even harder.

"I would need to be able to check out your story before I gave you any money," he said. "Are you willing to meet?"

"Not if you're going to have those men shoot at me again."

"What men?"

"You know. You've already buried two of them." And for that she felt a twinge of regret. But it had been their lives or hers and Jake's.

Jake...

She heard him murmur and call out in his sleep. He would be awake soon. Then she would have to put him back to sleep, because she had an appointment to keep.

"An hour and a half—at your warehouse," she said. Unfortunately, it was already after hours, so there would be nobody else around but Tom and his men. And her...

"And if anything happens to me," she added, "a copy of that flash drive will go to the police."

She didn't wait for him to agree or disagree. She

clicked off the cell and dropped it back into her purse—just in time—as Jake stumbled out of the bedroom looking all scruffy and sexy.

He would be furious if he knew what she'd done. But she was doing it for him as much as she was for herself and their baby. Because she wanted to be with him...

Tom hurled his cell phone across the room where it struck his office wall and broke into pieces. He hated being played. And he was definitely being played.

Either by Lillian Davies or her dimwit brother.

Neither of them was going to get away with it. If that flash drive existed, he would get it. And then he would kill them both. She'd told him not to have his men at the warehouse.

But he had no intention of walking into whatever trap she and that damn brother of hers and her Rambo bounty hunter thought they were setting for him.

Hell, no.

Tom Kuipers was nobody's fool.

He would set a trap for her instead. He used his desk phone to call his chief of security. "I have two meetings tonight," he told Archie Wells. "In the ware-house."

And his anger ebbed away as he realized that Lillian Davies and her brother had actually given him a gift—even if that flash drive didn't exist. He didn't have to worry about tracking either of them down. They were coming to him.

And to their deaths...

Chapter 21

"Were you talking to someone earlier?" Jake asked, and he looked around to see if she had her cell phone in the kitchen. But he saw only plates, which she'd already piled high with linguine noodles and pasta sauce. Chunks of bread, liberally buttered and peppered with cheese and garlic, perched on the edge of each plate.

His stomach growled.

And this time he was hungry for the food. Making love to her had worked up his appetite. It had also exhausted him to the point that he'd fallen asleep.

He couldn't believe he'd done that, not when he'd already been suspicious of her. And when he'd overheard her talking in the kitchen, he had jerked awake, afraid that she was no longer alone, that she was in danger and he'd been too distracted to protect her.

But when he'd walked out of the bedroom, his gun drawn, he'd found her alone.

She glanced up from the plates. "What did you hear?" she asked, and she sounded nervous. Or guilty.

He narrowed his eyes and studied her flushed face. "What was there to hear?"

She laughed. "Just some very terrible singing."

"It didn't sound like singing."

"I told you it was terrible."

"I find it hard to believe that you're terrible at anything," he said.

Hadn't he heard her sing before? In the shower, before he'd stepped inside and joined her…

And after he'd joined her, her singing had turned to moans and cries of pleasure.

So maybe he hadn't really heard her sing before. Or at least not long enough that he would be able to remember if she was a good or a bad singer.

"Before you claim that I'm not terrible at anything, you will want to try this meal," she warned him as she carried the plates to the small table in the eat-in area of the kitchen.

"You're an excellent cook," he said. "But you shouldn't have gone to all this trouble."

"I couldn't handle any more greasy burgers from that diner," she said. Then she patted her belly. "And neither could he."

He held out a chair for her. "This certainly looks healthier."

Before she sat down, she swapped the plates on the table. "This one has less on it," she said of the plate she took for herself.

"You're the one eating for two," he reminded her.

"But the bigger the baby gets, the less room I have for food," she said, and she patted her belly.

"You're really not that big," he assured her. It was just that her frame was so slender and delicate that the swell of her belly was especially noticeable. And beautiful.

She shook her head. "You don't have to charm me anymore, Jake."

"Anymore?"

"Like you did when we first met," she said.

Had he charmed her then? Even knowing who her family was, he'd been so drawn to her—to her beauty, to her sweetness. He hadn't tried to con her. He'd meant every word he'd told her then. And now.

But maybe she knew him too well to be charmed anymore. Since he'd told her about his dad and mom, she knew him better than anyone else ever had. And she hadn't called him a hypocrite for acting the way he had about her family.

She could have called him that and so many other things. But she was Lillian. Sweet Lillian.

"Eat," she urged him, "before it gets cold."

He was hungry, especially after making love with her. He'd been panting like he'd run a marathon before he fell asleep. His stomach growled again, so he dug in to his plate, twirling pasta around his fork. Then he shoveled it into his mouth.

"Is it good?" she asked.

He nodded. He wasn't about to tell her that it would have been better with fresh ingredients. There was an odd, almost metallic, flavor to it, but he had no idea how old the can of sauce was that she'd found in the cupboard. The bread was good, though. He used that to sop up the sauce, and he continued to eat as if he was ravenous.

She barely touched her food. Maybe it was like she'd said—she didn't have that much room for it with the baby taking up most of her stomach space. But it wasn't just that she wasn't eating, it was the way she was watching him.

And he knew—she hadn't been singing in the kitchen like she'd claimed. She had been talking to someone, like he'd suspected. The guilt was on her pretty face and in her blue eyes as she refused to meet his gaze.

"Lillian…" he murmured, but his words slurred together as if he'd been drinking. "What did you do?"

The question echoed within his head, the words sounding as distorted as she suddenly appeared to him. Her beautiful face wavered in and out of focus.

He tried to jump up from his chair as he realized what she'd done. "You drugged…" His legs wouldn't hold his weight. They buckled beneath him, and he dropped to the floor.

She'd drugged him. And he could think of only one reason why: to get away from him.

But then he couldn't think any more as he lost consciousness entirely.

Had she killed him?

Lillian hadn't been sure how many pills to crush up into his sauce. Had she given him too many?

Lillian dropped to her knees beside Jake and felt for his pulse. It beat quickly beneath her fingertips. And his chest—his magnificent muscular chest—rose and fell with deep breaths.

He was alive.

He was just sleeping. And since she had no idea how long he would stay asleep, she needed to leave quickly. She reached into one of his jeans pockets, feeling around for the keys to the rental.

Now a soft groan slipped through his parted lips, and his body tensed.

She froze.

Had she awakened him?

Then she saw his erection pushing against the fly of his jeans, and she smiled. She had only awakened part of him. But would he want her anymore after what she'd done? He might never forgive her for drugging him.

"I'm sorry," she whispered, and she pressed a kiss to his lips.

He murmured again, and it was as if he tried to drag his eyes open but the lids refused to lift. His thick dark lashes lay yet against his chiseled cheeks. He was still unconscious, but not completely.

She needed to hurry. She pushed her hand in his other pocket and finally found the keys. Good. She wouldn't have to waste time trying to remember how to hot-wire the SUV. She pulled the keys out and noticed his holster.

Should she take his gun?

It wasn't as if she actually knew how to shoot it, despite those long ago lessons Gran had given her. But Tom Kuipers wouldn't know that. Could she threaten him with it? But then if she took it, she left Jake totally unprotected.

Of course, with as unconscious as he was, he was completely vulnerable. Tears stung her eyes.

This had been a bad idea.

But she was committed now. And she knew if Jake was awake, there was no way he would let her go through with her plan to meet Mr. Kuipers. If she could record her former boss admitting that he had framed her, it would be nearly as good as the evidence she had downloaded to that flash drive.

His verbal confession would have to be enough to get the charges against her dropped. She had a record feature on her cell phone; she could use that to take down his statement. But how would she get him talking?

The gun?

She reached for the holster but then jerked her hand back when Jake moved. No. She did not need the gun. She needed to get to the warehouse before Jake woke up and stopped her. She knew her plan was as dangerous as Jake had warned her it was. But she had to risk it.

For her baby. And for Jake.

Because he was unconscious and couldn't hear her, she leaned forward and just before brushing her lips over his, she whispered, "I love you."

She didn't want him to know that, though. Not when she didn't think he returned her feelings. And even if he did, they had no guarantee of a future. Not until she got the charges against her dropped.

And this plan was her last-ditch effort for that. It could be her last attempt at anything, though.

She may not come back to Jake again.

Donny struggled against the bindings on his wrists. He would have shouted but one of the men who'd grabbed him had shoved a bandanna into his mouth after the first time he'd yelled.

Or actually, he'd screamed, probably sounding like a little girl. But these guys were huge.

His heart pumped fast and hard with fear. Were these Kuipers's men? If they were, he didn't like his chances for escaping. Not with as tightly as they'd bound his wrists and ankles.

Finally, the truck stopped, and the driver told the man sitting in the back with Donny, "Bring him along."

"Are you sure this is the place?" the guy in the passenger's seat asked.

They were all big, all with deep black hair and green eyes. They must have been brothers. Not that Donny looked like his brothers. With his thin blond hair and blue eyes, he looked like Lillian and their mother had.

The driver nodded. "Yeah."

"But he didn't tell you where he was hiding out."

Was Tom Kuipers hiding out? Maybe someone else had reported him to the authorities. Or he'd pissed off the wrong people the way Jake Howard had. The bounty hunter was relentless.

Surely, he would help Lillian.

If he believed her.

Maybe if Jake saw the flash drive, he would. But Donny didn't have it anymore.

"Should we see if he's here first—before we drag him along?" the guy in the back asked.

"Why do you two always doubt me?" the driver asked with a long-suffering sigh. He opened the door and stepped out. And despite their arguments, the other two followed suit. Then someone reached in and dragged out Donny.

With his ankles bound, he nearly fell over. But these guys were so much bigger than him that they easily lifted him. Two of them stood on either side of him, clasping his elbows to carry him. His bound feet dangled a foot or so above the ground.

"This one," the driver said as he stopped outside an apartment door. Instead of knocking, he drew his gun from his holster.

And Donny's heart beat faster. Just what the hell was going on?

The guy knocked. Several times.

"Maybe he's not here," one of the other men remarked.

The driver tilted his head as if he was listening. Then the others tensed and reached for their weapons. And finally, Donny heard it, too—a loud thud, like something or someone had fallen over.

"Shane?" one addressed the driver.

Shane nodded and kicked open the door. Then he cursed and rushed into the apartment. "Ryan, clear it!" he yelled out.

Donny couldn't see very far inside the doorway. He couldn't see much beyond the broken wood dangling from the jamb. The guy who must have been Ryan followed Shane inside, his gun drawn. With him out of the way, Donny could see a little more— like Shane dropping to his knees.

What the hell was going on? What had made the loud thud?

"The rest of the place is empty," Ryan called out as he stepped back into Donny's sight.

The guy who was still holding on to Donny murmured, "What the hell—"

But he wasn't looking inside; he was looking at Donny. "Just how much damn trouble is your sister in?" he asked.

"What do you mean?"

The man gestured inside the apartment again. And Donny turned back to look inside, and now he saw why Shane had dropped onto the floor. He knelt next to the prone body of Jake Howard.

"Those guys must have knocked out Howard and grabbed your sister," his captor told him.

Knocked Jake out or killed him?

The big bounty hunter wasn't moving. And probably the only way someone would have gotten Lillian away from Jake Howard was over his dead body.

Chapter 22

Something cold and hard and wet struck Jake, jerking him awake with a curse slipping out of his lips. Instinctively, he reached for his holster, but it was empty. And he lay, vulnerable, on the floor, staring up at three huge guys.

How the hell had they gotten the jump on him? Then he remembered Lillian's dinner and how she'd drugged him.

Lillian!

He didn't even look for her, though. He knew she was gone. If she hadn't left already, these guys might have taken her for the bounty. But they weren't heading to the jail with her. They were still here, staring down at him. He'd forgotten just how damn big the O'Hanigans were.

Shane held his gun out to him, handle first. "I

took this—just in case you reached for it and started shooting before you identified us."

"He might have started shooting because he recognized us," Trick added with a smirk.

"What happened?" another man asked, his voice higher than any of the O'Hanigans. Donny Davies stumbled forward, his ankles bound as well as his wrists.

And Jake knew why the O'Hanigans had tracked him down, although he wasn't quite sure how they'd managed to find the US Marshals' safe house and Donny Davies so quickly. He'd seriously underestimated the bounty-hunting brothers.

"Where's my sister?" Donny asked, his voice cracking with concern. "What happened to her?"

"Yeah, what happened?" Shane O'Hanigan asked. "Did some of those armed guys knock you out?"

Jake's face flushed. "No."

"You were out cold," Ryan said, "until we threw that ice water on you."

Jake picked up a cube that was melting on his chest. "You could have spared me the ice." The frozen cubes had hurt, but it had been effective in finally rousing him. He had been struggling to wake himself up ever since Lillian had taken off. But every time he'd managed to get to his feet, he'd fallen over again.

"What happened?" Shane persisted. But even as he asked the question, he glanced over at the food on the table, and a smile curved his mouth. "She drugged you!"

Jake wasn't sure where she'd found the sleeping pills, but she must have.

Shane shook his head. "You should have brought her in right away. Now you have to give up your sweet ride, and you don't even have the bounty anymore."

"I know where she is." Or he could guess. He jumped up, but he was still a little woozy and might have fallen over again if not for Shane grabbing his arm and steadying him.

"On a plane to a country with no extradition to the US," Trick said.

"She played you," Ryan added with a chuckle.

She had—with the food and the drugs. But he didn't think it was because she'd wanted to escape him.

"My sister's not like that," Donny protested. "She's not a con artist."

"Then she would be the only one in your family who isn't," Shane said with a derisive snort. "What makes her so special?"

Everything, Jake wanted to say. But right now he was furious—with Lillian and most especially with Donny. He grabbed the younger man by the shirt and dragged him close. "What the hell did you do with that flash drive?"

Donny's face flushed.

"When we grabbed him, he was claiming it never existed," Shane said. "That there is no such thing."

And Jake's stomach plummeted. Had he been played? Had it all been a lie to convince him not to bring her to jail? Maybe she'd conned him for payback—like she felt he'd conned her eight months ago. And even though he'd had it coming, he was devastated.

* * *

The company gates stood open, but Lillian hesitated before driving the SUV through them. Once she drove back beyond the offices to the area where the warehouses were, she could get locked inside those gates or in that warehouse. And she might never leave.

Alive.

Jake had been right. This was a bad idea. One that could get her and their baby killed. As if the baby felt her fear, he kicked—hard. And maybe that kick knocked some sense into Lillian because she shifted the transmission into Reverse. But before she could back away from those gates, a white van pulled up behind her, blocking her in. And the doors of the SUV were jerked open.

The guy on the passenger's side pointed a gun across the console at her while the guy on the driver's side pulled her from her seat. She stumbled and nearly fell, and, since she hadn't put it in Park, the SUV rolled back into the van.

She gasped.

"Don't worry about it," the guy said. "The vehicle is the least of your concerns right now. The boss has been waiting for you. And for that flash drive."

Lillian didn't doubt that. He wanted to make sure no evidence existed to implicate him in the embezzlement. She wasn't sure if the evidence existed or not anymore, either. So she had to make sure she got more. That part of her plan might still work. The part she should have worked out better before she'd driven to the company building was how she would escape once she obtained that evidence.

The guy jerked her forward again, pulling her toward one of the warehouses that were behind the fence, behind the company's office building. Lillian had always thought the warehouses were used only to store the building equipment that Kuipers's wife and father-in-law sold. But now she knew a lot more than storage happened in those warehouses.

Or was about to happen. Secret meetings like this one. She doubted it was the only one Tom Kuipers had had here. Was this where he'd met with the men he'd ordered to kill her?

Was this where she was going to die?

The baby kicked her belly, and that kick reminded Lillian of everything she had to fight for.

The baby.

Jake.

If he would ever forgive her. And she doubted that he would. He had to be furious with her for drugging him, for sneaking out…

Did he think that she had done all of that just to escape him? Did he think that she'd planned it all along so that she could remain on the run with the money she'd stolen?

She should have left him a note. She should have explained…

She didn't want to die with him thinking that she'd used and deceived him. So she couldn't die. She wouldn't die. She would fight.

With the man dragging her along, they'd crossed the asphalt quickly to the open side door of one of the warehouses. She would have preferred that the big door was open, since it would have been easier to escape.

Maybe she could hit one of the switches that activated it.

The man tightly grasped her arm, though, so when they passed through the service door, she couldn't reach the panel for the big doors, even though it was close. Just a foot or more from the service door. But she couldn't reach it with her free arm because in that hand she grasped something else. Something she couldn't put down until she got Tom Kuipers's confession on it.

She fumbled with her phone, hitting the record switch. Maybe it would have been smarter to call 911. But she hadn't wanted them to show up too soon and arrest her before she could get the evidence to clear her name. She needed Tom's confession before she could call for help.

But she didn't even see Tom yet.

Had he ever intended to show up? Or had he just ordered these men to kill her? After the way they'd shot up the cottage and tried running them off the road, they might have had orders to shoot on sight. She wouldn't put it past Tom to have given them those orders. Then he could blame her death on someone else. Just like he'd blamed his stealing on her.

"I came here to meet with Mr. Kuipers," she told the man dragging her across the floor.

The guy pitched his voice low and murmured, "That was crazy, lady. You should have kept running."

But Tom would have kept chasing her. And so would have the authorities and the bounty hunters.

And what would Jake have done? Would he have brought her to jail or would he have run with her? She hadn't been able to trust him enough to find out.

Trust would always be an issue for them—on both sides. He would struggle to trust her and she him. So she couldn't fight for a future with Jake.

They didn't have a chance for one. She had to fight for a future for their baby.

Pain gripped her, clutching at her stomach. She bent over and groaned.

"What the hell…" the guy murmured. And he finally released her and stepped back.

Here was Lillian's chance to try to escape. But when she whirled around to head back to that service door, someone blocked the opening.

Tom Kuipers stepped forward and chuckled. "Long time no see, Lillian." His gaze skimmed up and down her body. "You've gained a little weight since the last time I saw you."

"I'm pregnant," she said. Not that she thought that would make a difference to him.

He wasn't going to spare her life because she was about to bring another life into the world. That pain gripped her belly again, and she grimaced.

She couldn't be in labor, though. It was too soon. Maybe she was just sick over what she'd done to Jake and over the mistake she'd made in coming here. It couldn't be for nothing, though.

She grasped her phone carefully, making sure that the microphone on it pointed toward her former employer. She had to catch every word he said, hoping that he would incriminate himself.

She didn't have to wait long.

He continued, "Maybe that was why it was so easy to frame you for embezzling that money."

Bingo.

She had it. Everything she needed to prove her innocence.

But still he kept talking, "Now I know why you spent so much time in the bathroom, which gave me so much time at your desk to put all that evidence into place for the police and the prosecutor."

This was almost as good as the flash drive. If only she had that, too.

But she couldn't count on that, and she never should have counted on her brother. She had everything she needed now, except a way to escape.

Tom moved away from the side door, but he stepped closer to her. His eyes narrowed and he studied her face now instead of her body. "You were so naive and trusting that you made it easy for me."

She'd been the same way with Jake. Too naive. Too trusting.

"Just like your showing up here," he continued. "You've made it so easy for me to get rid of you once and for all."

She flinched. And it wasn't just because another cramp gripped her stomach. "If you kill me, the police will look into my murder. They'll figure out the truth."

He snorted disparagingly. "They haven't managed that yet."

"They will," she said. "If anything happens to me, they'll get that flash drive…"

Tom snorted again. "Yeah, that's what your brother claimed when he called me. But you know…"

She held her breath as another wave of pain gripped her.

"I don't think that flash drive ever existed," he

said. "You're just not smart enough to have collected evidence against me."

She couldn't defend herself against his criticism. She hadn't been very smart to show up here. But she could escape. She had to.

"And if you had any evidence," Tom continued as he walked around her, "then you'd be at the police department turning it over to them. Not here."

That was true. "My brother has it," she said. "He will turn it in for me."

Tom shook his head. "No. He promised it to me. For a price."

She gasped with shock. But she shouldn't have been surprised. She'd suspected for a while now that Donny had betrayed her.

"Of course, he already sold it to me once," Tom said. "But he didn't produce it."

So he had betrayed Tom Kuipers, too.

"Your family really is a bunch of degenerates," Tom said.

"That's why you hired me," she said. "So you could set me up to take the fall for your crime."

He nodded. "Of course. And given your family's reputation, no one will suspect the truth."

They would, if she could get her recording out of the warehouse. She waited until he circled around her again. Then she started edging toward the open door. If she could get through it.

And the gates.

But she didn't get but a few feet away before a hand grasped her hair and jerked her back.

"Where do you think you're going?" Tom asked her. "You came here to sell me that flash drive.

Where is it?" He grabbed both her arms and pulled her hands toward him. And the phone dropped from her grasp. He laughed as he saw that it had been recording. "So that was your plan?"

It had been stupid. She saw that now. Jake had been right. Even with his help, it wouldn't have worked.

Tom Kuipers stomped hard on the phone, breaking the screen and crunching the plastic between his boot and the concrete floor.

Lillian knew she had just lost her last shot at proving her innocence. But that was the least of her concerns now, when Tom ordered the men, "Now kill her…"

Tom was a heartless son of a bitch and damn proud of it. But for some reason, he didn't want to be the one to pull the trigger anymore. He didn't even want to see it—when one of his men put a bullet in Lillian Davies's brain.

He'd had no problem framing her for his crime, no problem sending her to prison. But killing her…

Maybe if she hadn't been pregnant.

And scared and vulnerable.

There was something about the woman, something that made a man feel protective, even when he wasn't the protective type. That must have been why, instead of bringing her to jail, the bounty hunter had started protecting her.

Tom wasn't going to protect her, though. He wanted her dead. He just didn't want to do it himself anymore. He'd almost made it to the door when someone called out, "Mr. Kuipers?"

It wasn't her. She wasn't begging for her life. It was one of the men.

Tom turned back. "What?"

"I—I thought you wanted to do this yourself." The guy gestured at Lillian.

That was what he'd been saying.

And if he changed his mind now, the men might think he'd gone soft. Hell, he had to do it himself. He had to pull the trigger—or he risked his guys disrespecting him and questioning his authority. He couldn't have that. He needed their respect.

But more than that, he needed their fear.

"Yeah," he said. "I'll do it." And he reached for his weapon.

Chapter 23

Each ring of the phone increased the tension that already gripped Jake. Why the hell wasn't he answering?

Did he not want the flash drive anymore? Maybe he didn't believe it existed—like Jake had started to think until Shane O'Hanigan had handed it over—in exchange for Jake's car. He would have given his life for that flash drive if it would save Lillian's.

Was he too late?

He had no idea how long Lillian had been gone. How long he'd been out before the O'Hanigans had thrown that ice water in his face.

They stood around him yet, probably waiting for him to bring them to the Nova. He didn't want to do that, though. Once they saw the condition it was in, they would probably want out of his deal.

And he couldn't give back that flash drive. He had plans for it. He was so damn glad that Shane hadn't believed Donny lying about not having it. Apparently, the O'Hanigans had held him upside down until it had fallen out of his pocket.

"Where the hell are you?" The question emanated from the cell phone pressed to Jake's ear.

It wasn't his cell. It was Donny's.

"You're late for the meeting you requested," the voice continued in a low snarl.

Jake looked at Donny, whose face was flushed. Maybe that was because he continued to struggle against the bindings at his wrists and ankles. Jake hadn't had the O'Hanigans cut him loose yet. And now he never wanted to free the guy. He wanted to kill him.

"Your sister showed up, though," Tom Kuipers continued.

Jake's heart slammed against his chest. She had gone there. He felt a twinge of guilt that he'd doubted her, that he had thought, even for a moment, that she might have been lying to him.

"She's not my sister." Jake finally spoke.

She was the mother of his child. If she was still alive...

And if she wasn't alive, the baby wouldn't have survived, either.

Panic gripped him, stealing his breath away, but he fought it back. He had to stay focused.

"Who the hell is this?" Kuipers asked.

"The man who has what you want," Jake replied. Hopefully, Kuipers still had what he wanted.

Kuipers snorted. "Donny Davies? I don't want him."

"No. You want the flash drive he has," Jake said.

There was a long silence. "He sold you that fantasy, too?"

"It's real," Jake said. And he glanced down at the plastic device in his hand. "And I have it."

"I've already paid for that thing once," Tom said. Then he lowered his voice to a mutter and remarked, "And a new cell phone." Then louder and more emphatically, he added, "I'm not buying it again."

"I don't want money," Jake said. "I want Lillian Davies."

There was another long pause before Kuipers replied, "What makes you think I know where the hell she is?"

"You just said she showed up," Jake reminded the lying son of a bitch. "Like her brother, she set up a meeting with you, too."

Jake never should have believed that she was singing in the kitchen. He never should have trusted her. And he wouldn't make that mistake again.

But as furious as he was with her, he didn't want anything to happen to her or to their baby.

"And you let her come alone…" Kuipers made a tsking noise in the phone.

Jake sucked in a breath that burned his lungs. She had definitely met him. "You better not have hurt her," he warned the man. "Or the authorities getting a hold of this flash drive will be the least of your concerns."

Jake would take the man apart—literally—if he'd harmed Lillian.

"If you want to work a deal, you shouldn't be

threatening me," Kuipers said, and he made that tsking noise in the phone again.

"Deal?" Jake asked.

"You claim to have something I want," Kuipers said. "And it sounds like I have something you want."

"Is she okay?" Jake asked.

Kuipers chuckled. "I wondered if you were after the bounty. Now I know—it's the baby."

"Baby?" he asked. It hadn't been born, had it? Lillian wasn't due for weeks yet, though, so of course it hadn't been born.

"Is it your baby?" Kuipers asked. "Is that why you kept risking your life for her?"

Jake didn't want the man to know how much leverage he had over him, so he didn't answer. But he couldn't stop himself from asking, "Are Lillian and the baby okay?"

"You can see for yourself when you show up here," Kuipers said.

"Where is here?" Jake asked.

"I thought you knew she was meeting me?" Kuipers asked, and now there was suspicion in his voice. "So you should damn well know where."

"His warehouse," Donny whispered. "That's where he'd want to meet her. That's where I was supposed to meet him."

"Your warehouse," Jake said. "I'll meet you there. And Lillian better be fine." He would have demanded to speak with her, but he didn't get the chance.

Kuipers disconnected the call.

"What the hell are you thinking?" Shane asked. "You're walking into a trap. And I do mean walking—you don't have a ride anymore."

No. He didn't. Not since Lillian had taken off in the rental.

"If you want your ride," Jake said, "you have to drive me to that warehouse."

Shane shook his head. "That wasn't part of the deal." He gestured at Donny and the device in Jake's hand. "We delivered. Now it's time for you to deliver."

"I will," Jake said. But he needed help—their help—to get Lillian back. "After I meet Kuipers at the warehouse…"

"You won't be alive to give us a car then," Shane said. "The guy wants to kill you—like I'm sure he already killed Lillian Davies."

Jake sucked in a breath. But he couldn't argue that; Shane was probably right. Tom Kuipers had probably shot Lillian on sight, like he'd had his men try to shoot her and him so many times before.

His heart ached with loss. But even if she was gone, he had to bring her killer to justice and clear her name.

He owed her and their child that. Their baby…

He couldn't think about everything he might have lost, though. He had to stay focused. "Come on, Shane." It was as close to begging as he would come.

Shane shook his head. "This is why you don't get involved with women, man."

Jake couldn't argue that with him. But it was too late. He'd already fallen for Lillian.

"They make you act crazy," Shane said, "make you risk your life."

Jake had no life without Lillian.

But then the oldest O'Hanigan sighed. "Damn it. We'll go with you."

"Shane?" Trick questioned his brother.

Shane shrugged. "We can't let him go off alone."

Like Lillian had gone off alone.

"We could get killed, too," Ryan said.

Shane snorted. "Not a chance. No matter what Tuttle thinks, we're better than Jake."

Jake was beginning to think the O'Hanigans were. Lillian probably wouldn't have been able to drug them and escape. Hopefully, she could manage to escape Kuipers—if it wasn't already too late for her.

And if it was too late, Jake wasn't certain what he would do. He would need the O'Hanigans there to stop him from becoming what his father was—a killer.

Lillian released the breath she'd been holding since Tom Kuipers had turned around earlier and walked back toward her, his gun drawn. She had already braced herself, waiting for the shot to sound, to penetrate her body...

But instead of the gunshot ringing out, Kuipers's phone rang. And rang.

He'd taken a long time to answer it. And once he had, she knew to whom he'd talked: Jake.

How had he gotten Tom Kuipers's private cell number? But then he was Jake: he had his ways and would use whatever means necessary to get what he wanted.

Just as he had with her.

But was she what he wanted this time?

And why? Could he possibly return her feelings? Or was he only after the bounty on her like he'd been with her dad and oldest brother? After she'd drugged him, she couldn't blame him. He had to be furious with her.

Tom Kuipers reached out and grasped her hair like he had before. He jerked her forward and stared into her face. "Does that damn flash drive really exist?" he asked. "Or has it all been a scam hatched by you and your brother?"

"That wasn't my brother on the phone," she said. She'd only heard his side of the conversation, but somehow she knew it was Jake who had called him.

Maybe because Tom Kuipers's body had tensed, and there was a look in his beady eyes now—a fearful look. She'd seen Jake put that look on men's faces before when her dad and brother Dave had discovered he was the man she was dating eight months ago.

Tom shook his head. "No. That wasn't your idiot brother."

"Jake."

"He claims he has the flash drive. Is he lying?"

He could have been. She wasn't sure how he would have gotten it. They hadn't been able to find Donny.

But because she wanted Tom Kuipers to believe her, she answered with as much of the truth as she could share with him, "I broke into your office shortly after my arrest. I downloaded the files that clear my name to that flash drive." She swallowed hard as regret and betrayal overwhelmed her. Then she continued, "And I entrusted it to my brother to get it to my lawyer."

Kuipers laughed. "You are a fool. And so is this bounty hunter friend of yours." He looked up from her face to focus on his guys. "Make damn sure this bounty hunter doesn't get away from you again. I want him dead."

Lillian cried out, but it wasn't just with fear for Jake's life. She cried out as pain clenched her stomach. Then fluid rushed between her legs as her water broke.

Her baby was coming.

But it was too soon. Yet, even if she'd carried the baby to full-term, his chance of survival was slim. Lillian had no doubt that Tom Kuipers intended to kill her, Jake and their baby...

Donny rubbed his thumb over the marks on his wrists where the zip ties had cut into his skin during his struggle to escape. Finally, the O'Hanigan brothers had released him. But Donny no longer wanted to escape them.

Instead, he'd begged to go with them—and Jake—to rescue his sister. But none of the men—Jake included—looked like they were going to a rescue. Their faces grim, they looked like they were heading to a funeral.

Theirs?

Or Lillian's?

Was it too late to save her?

Donny didn't want to believe that because, if it was, it was all his fault. He should have done what she'd asked of him. Lillian had always asked so little of everyone in her life.

He sat in the third-row seat, way in the back, of the Suburban that Shane O'Hanigan, the oldest of the three brothers, was driving, while Jake sat in the passenger's seat next to him. Donny had figured out who they all were now. Despite there being another seat, and Trick and Ryan O'Hanigan, between them, Donny could feel Jake's anger and concern.

Guilt overwhelming him, a sob slipped between his lips. Trick and Ryan turned around, but Shane only glanced in the rearview mirror. Jake wouldn't look at him, though.

Maybe he couldn't.

Donny didn't think he would ever be able to look in a mirror again. How he would hate what he saw. He hated the man he had become. And his mother would have hated him, too. She would have hated what he'd done to his sister—and all of it just for money.

"You didn't have to come along," Ryan told him.

"And you can stay in the vehicle if you're scared," Trick added.

Donny was scared but not for himself. Well, at least not just for himself. He was scared for Lillian. And he could tell that Jake Howard was, too. And that, a man like Jake Howard being scared, scared Donny more than anything else ever had.

"I'm worried about my sister," he said.

"You should have been worried when she got arrested," Jake said. "And you should have turned over that flash drive to her lawyer like she asked you to."

He should have. He couldn't argue with Jake or defend himself. What he'd done was indefensible. He would never forgive himself.

And he might not even be able to ask Lillian to forgive him.

Chapter 24

Jake knew he was walking into a trap. He'd already told Donny as much when the young man had insisted on walking through those gates with him. The guy clearly felt badly over what he'd done—or had failed to do—to help his sister. He wanted to help her now, though, even though they were both well aware they might be too late.

His stomach churned and not just with all the drugs Lillian had fed him. The thought of her already being dead sickened Jake. He couldn't have lost her again.

And their child...

He couldn't let himself think about the baby. Not now. He had to focus or they would all wind up dead.

"When we get in there," Jake told Donny, "you find Lillian and get her to safety."

Donny met his gaze. His face was pale. All the

color had drained from it, leaving his eyes—blue eyes like Lillian's—stark with fear. But despite that fear, he didn't back down. He just nodded, but his throat moved as if he was struggling to swallow down that fear or more sobs.

On the way to the warehouse, Jake had hatched a plan with the O'Hanigans. It wasn't a great plan, but it had a shot at working. But it would all be for nothing if Lillian was already dead.

She couldn't be...

He refused to accept that. He refused to accept that he'd lost her and their baby.

Donny drew in a deep breath and nodded again. "Okay, let's do this."

They didn't have a choice. There was no backing out now. Guards surrounded them the second they stepped through those open gates.

The men peered around them.

"You came on foot?" one of them skeptically asked.

"Uber," Jake said.

Shane O'Hanigan would get a kick out of that. And he was listening. He'd given Jake one of the two-way radios he used to communicate with his brothers when they were apprehending fugitives.

Since he'd left the US Marshals, Jake had worked alone. He preferred it. Then he didn't have to worry about anyone else. Just himself.

But in this case, he'd had no choice. He needed help. When Lillian had drugged him and taken off, she had left him no choice.

Kuipers's men weren't giving him a choice, either. After they patted him and Donny down for weapons, they pointed their guns at them. And the one who'd spoken first, the one with the gray hair in the military cut, spoke again. "Okay, smart-ass, get in here."

Another of the men pulled the gates closed and locked them, as if Jake had any intention of turning around and running for it.

Now, Donny…

He might have changed his mind about helping to rescue his sister. But if he had, it didn't show as he started forward at Jake's side. "Let's do this," he murmured, his voice cracking with fear.

And Jake felt a moment's hesitation and regret. When they'd hatched this plan, the O'Hanigans had called it a suicide mission. Donny knew that he was putting his life in jeopardy. But he didn't seem to mind now. He headed with purpose toward the open side door of the warehouse.

Like Jake, he wanted to see if Lillian was alive. Or if they'd arrived too late to save her.

They didn't have to wait until they saw her, though. Jake heard her scream.

"Run!" she hollered at them. "It's a trap!"

But the overhead doors were already opening, shots firing out at him and Donny. He shoved the other man toward the ground as he drew his weapon—the one he'd stashed in his boot where the guards hadn't looked. But before he could get off a shot, a bullet tore into his shoulder. Blood spurted his face as the wound burned. And he dropped to the ground next to Donny.

Lillian screamed again as she watched the blood spatter Jake's face before he dropped to the ground. His luck had finally run out. He'd been hit.

And it was all her fault. Maybe if she hadn't drugged him, his reflexes would have been faster. Hell, if she hadn't drugged him, she wouldn't be here, either—lying on the concrete floor of the warehouse.

She screamed as another contraction gripped her stomach. She felt as if she was being ripped in half. And her heart had already been ripped out when she'd watched Jake get struck and fall.

More men fell—in the warehouse—as more shots rang out. These shots came from outside, though, as a big Suburban crashed through the gates and drove toward the building. Barrels pointed out the windows of the vehicle as the men in it fired on the warehouse.

"Get up," a voice said, close to her ear as a man bent over her. "We need to get the hell out of here."

Donny!

She struggled to move, but another contraction hit. And Donny shouted, "She's in labor."

Going into labor was probably what had saved her life so far. For some reason, all the men had hesitated over shooting a pregnant woman, especially one who was about to bring a life into the world. But if her baby was born now, he might be giving up his life for hers.

Just as Jake might have.

"Donny," she said. But all the gunfire drowned out her voice. Then sirens wailed over them.

Someone must have reported the gunfire and called 911. But it was too late.

For Jake.

And for Tom Kuipers. He'd slipped out of the

warehouse a while ago. Even as he'd set up a trap for Jake, he'd probably suspected that Jake might have been setting one of his own. Had Jake called the police? Were the men in the Suburban working with Jake?

If so, they should have showed up sooner—before he'd been shot.

"Hang in there," Donny implored her as he pushed her tangled hair back from her sweaty face. "Help's coming."

Help was too late for her baby. She knew there was no stopping her labor now. She could only hope that it wasn't too late for Jake. She murmured his name just as strong arms lifted her.

She tensed. Was it one of the men? Were they dragging her away like they'd dragged her into the warehouse earlier? Were they bringing her to wherever Mr. Kuipers had gone? She swung out, trying to fight off the man.

And he cursed. His voice was familiar. It was Jake. She glanced up into his face. The spatters of blood had trickled down his cheek, leaving red smears. And his shoulder, where the bullet had entered, was torn, the shirt and his skin beneath the shirt. Both were soaked with blood.

"Put me down," she told him even as she panted for breath. "You're hurt."

And carrying her would only injure him more.

But he didn't exhibit any weakness or pain as he rushed out of the warehouse with her clasped tightly in his arms.

"We need to get her to the hospital," he said as

Donny opened the door to the Suburban that had raced up to the warehouse.

"Looks like you need a doctor more," the driver remarked. It was the guy Jake had struck over the head on the deck outside his safe house. Shane O'Hanigan did not appear to be harboring a grudge, though, since he'd acted as Jake's backup.

"She's in labor," Donny said.

The driver cursed. "An ambulance is on its way."

But it wouldn't arrive in time. And Jake must have realized the same thing. He helped her into the middle row of seats and ordered Shane O'Hanigan, "Drive! Hurry!"

The driver did as he was told, but he cursed as he pulled out of the parking lot. "I'll leave Ryan and Trick here. But you and I are going to be in trouble for leaving the scene."

"We'll explain later," Jake said. And he reached out, squeezing her hand as she cried out with another contraction. Blood streaked down his arm from his shoulder wound.

He had to be hurting just as badly as she was. He had a bullet in him. So it was good they weren't waiting around to give reports to the police. They needed to head straight to the hospital—for Jake.

Would the doctors be able to save the baby, though?

"Ryan's got the flash drive to turn over to the police. But we need to make sure Kuipers doesn't get away," Shane O'Hanigan remarked.

"It's too late," Lillian said between pants for breath. "He got away."

And because of that, she would never be safe.

* * *

If only he hadn't stopped in the office to grab his briefcase.

But he'd had no choice. The tickets were in there, the ones for the private plane that didn't need to file flight manifests. Nobody would have known where he'd gone, if he'd been able to get away in time.

But he hadn't moved fast enough. And now police officers surrounded his Porsche. He thought about just continuing to drive—straight through them. But their weapons were raised, pointing directly through his windshield at his head. If he tried to get away, they would fire at him.

And trying to get away would only make him look guilty. But despite how things looked or whatever anyone claimed about him, there was no proof for the police to arrest him. So he stopped. Before he could open the door, though, it was jerked open. He was pulled from the vehicle and pushed over the hood.

Hands ran over him in a quick but thorough search. They took his gun and his wallet and even his pocketknife.

"What's this about?" he asked, feigning outrage. "Why are you stopping me? I'm the victim. Lillian Davies robbed my company. Then she showed up here today, shooting…if my men killed her, it was only in self-defense."

And if they said anything different, he would kill them, too.

The officers were stone-faced, as if they couldn't hear him. That silence made him nervous. But it got much worse when one of them began to speak, as he read Tom his Miranda rights.

"What are you doing?" he shrieked. "I've done nothing wrong."

Except for sticking around as long as he had. He should have left when Lillian Davies had failed to make her court date. He should have known then that this was all going to go very wrong.

But it hadn't happened yet.

He still had hope that his plan would work—that he would get away with everything he'd done and most especially with all that money he'd taken. He had two tickets in that briefcase. One for himself and one for his hot young girlfriend.

Soon he would be living out every man's fantasy.

"You have no evidence against me," he told them. "I will sue you all for false arrest."

But then one of those officers held up a flash drive. And Tom knew.

Lillian Davies hadn't been lying. The flash drive was real. And it was all over for Tom. He could have tried bribing the officers if there had only been one or two. But five men led him from his Porsche to the back seat of a cruiser.

And he knew that the odds weren't in his favor. At least one of those five men was probably too honest to be bought. No. Tom would have to find another way out of these charges. But what would those charges be?

Just the embezzlement?

Or would there be murder charges, as well?

Had the guys killed Lillian Davies like he'd ordered them to? Just like he'd ordered them to kill that damn bounty hunter and her brother.

He cursed. Even if he faced two or three damn murder charges, he hoped like hell Lillian Davies and her damn bounty hunter were dead.

Chapter 25

Lillian's screams rang out from somewhere down the hall. That same panic that had gripped him when he'd awakened on the floor of the US Marshals' safe house with her gone gripped Jake again. Just like then, he had to find her. But feeling as groggy as he had when he'd awakened on that floor, he stumbled as he walked down the corridor.

He needed someone to throw ice water on him now. Or maybe he needed the blood the ER doctor had recommended after he'd stitched up Jake's shoulder.

Another scream rang out and Jake felt it as well as heard it. It reverberated inside his soul. But now he knew where she was and pushed open the door.

"Sir, you can't be in here," a nurse protested as she glanced up from the side of Lillian's bed.

But was it really a bed? Lillian wasn't resting. Her legs were up and she was curled over her belly. And when she looked up at him, her face was flushed a very dark red and tears streamed from her eyes. "Jake!"

He rushed to her side, the opposite side from the nurse who relaxed now that Lillian had called out his name. The woman had obviously thought he was just a patient who'd wandered into the wrong room. And with his bandaged shoulder, he looked like a patient.

If he hadn't passed out when they'd first arrived at the hospital, he wouldn't have bothered getting treatment. But he'd awakened on a gurney with a doctor stitching up his wound. At least the bullet had gone straight through and he hadn't been carted off to surgery when he'd been unconscious.

Instead of waking up to Lillian, like he'd wanted, Shane O'Hanigan had been next to his gurney.

"Did you pass out from the gunshot wound or from the fear of becoming a daddy?" Shane had goaded him.

"Blood loss," the doctor had replied for him, which had saved Jake from having to lie to a man that, despite their rivalry, was becoming a friend.

He was afraid of becoming a daddy. He had no example to follow except for one that had been tragically, criminally wrong. If he hadn't rushed outside and hidden beneath those pines in his backyard, his father would killed him, too.

Lillian reached out and clutched his hand in hers. "Jake, tell them it's too soon. The baby can't come now." Her voice broke with sobs and then another scream tore from her throat.

It was as if she was being tortured.

He glared at the nurse. But the nurse was not alone in the room. There was a doctor near Lillian's feet. And a doctor and another nurse stood in a corner of the room near an incubator and a bunch of machines. Their faces were grim, as if they all agreed it was too soon for the baby.

They were going to lose him or her.

Between Lillian's sobs, she murmured, "It's all my fault. My fault... I shouldn't have set up that meeting."

And Jake worried that if they lost the baby, he would lose Lillian, too. She would blame herself for whatever happened to their child.

"Shh," he said, trying to calm her fears, even as his own overwhelmed him. "This is our baby. This kid is strong and tough..." He brushed the sweat-soaked hair back from her face. "And beautiful, if she or he looks anything like you."

A faint smile curved her lips. But then her mouth twisted into a grimace and she cried out again. She sounded as if she was in agony.

And Jake wished he could take all her pain away.

The doctor looked up at her. "You have to push now, Ms. Davies," he said. "The baby's crowning."

Panic clutched Jake. "Is she right?" he asked the young doctor. "Is it too soon?"

"We can't stop her labor," the doctor said. "So the baby is coming *now*."

And now was immediate. With one push, the baby came out. Jake's heart flipped as he stared down at his son. He was little, but he was squalling.

"His lungs are developed," the doctor said. "I think he's a little more than thirty-six weeks."

That made sense since Jake had been seeing Lillian for about a month before her dad and brother had come back eight months ago.

"Do you want to cut the cord, Daddy?" the doctor asked.

Jake froze. And the doctor looked at Lillian, probably worried that he'd misspoken. She nodded before collapsing back against the bed.

His fingers shook, but he managed to squeeze the scissors the doctor handed to him, quickly clipping the cord so he could turn back toward Lillian.

"Are you okay?" he asked.

"Exhausted," the nurse answered for her, as she sponged off Lillian's sweaty forehead.

She rallied, trying to sit up to see the baby again. "Is the baby..."

The other doctor and nurse had already taken him—hooking him up to the machines they'd brought. That doctor, an older female, looked over at Lillian. "Like Daddy told you, he's strong. He's little but everything looks to be well developed. You have a healthy son."

Lillian released a ragged breath. "I knew it..." she murmured. "I knew he was a boy." She turned toward Jake. "You have a son."

"We have a son," he said.

The doctor and nurse beside Lillian finished up with her, making sure she was all right before settling her into the bed in a fresh gown. But she still did not relax—not even when the other doctor brought the baby to her. "Here's your son, Momma," she said.

Lillian stared down at him with so many emotions

swirling in her beautiful blue eyes. Jake experienced them all with her. The love and awe…

But the regret, too.

He felt a pang of fear as that look crossed her face. Then she held the baby out toward him. "Here, Jake."

He automatically reached for the infant, who was so small. "Don't you want to hold him?" he asked.

She shook her head and tears trailed down her face. "I can't. I can't get attached."

"What?" Jake asked. "What are you talking about?" The moment he'd seen the baby, he'd gotten attached. And it had been the same with her; when he'd literally and purposely run into her in that grocery store all those months ago, he'd fallen for her.

"You have to take him," she said, and her voice cracked with sobs. "You have to raise him. I'll be in jail."

Lillian's heart broke as the doctor and nurse wheeled the baby out of her room. They were just bringing him to the neonatal intensive care unit. They weren't taking him away permanently.

At least not yet. But when they brought him back to this room, it was possible that she might be gone, taken off to jail.

When everyone had left but Jake, he turned toward her and asked again, "What are you talking about?" And he looked horrified.

She could understand his hesitation, though. He might not have wanted to be a father at all, let alone a single father. "Don't you want him?" she asked.

"Of course I do," he replied. And there was no

hesitation now. Then he added, "But I don't want just him. I want you, too."

Her heart flipped in her chest. "Even after what I did?"

"I'm not happy you drugged me and put your life in danger," he said.

Heat rushed to her face. "That was stupid, so stupid." Regret overwhelmed her. Risking her own life had been bad enough, but risking their baby's, too, had been inexcusable. "I don't expect you to forgive me," she said. "Or to ever trust me again."

But where she was going, it wouldn't matter. She had no hope of a future, at least not for a long time.

"Will you be able to trust me again?" he asked.

She hadn't thought she could. But Jake had proven himself. He'd taken a bullet for her in order to rescue her. She reached out and gently skimmed her fingers over the bandage on his shoulder. "I'm sorry."

"I'm sorry," he said. "I did purposely set out to meet you so that I could find out where your dad and your brother were hiding. But everything else that happened…that wasn't on purpose. That was because I couldn't help but fall in—"

She pressed her fingers over his lips. "Don't say it," she pleaded. It would be easier for her to leave him if she didn't know that he actually returned her feelings. "Please, don't say it."

"Why not?" he asked against her fingers.

Her skin tingled, and she pulled her hand away from his mouth. "Because we have no future."

His dark eyes darkened more with pain. "You still can't trust me."

She shook her head. "We have no future because I'm going to jail."

He smiled, and now the pain was all hers. He found that amusing? But then he told her, "You're not going to jail. Donny gave the flash drive to the O'Hanigans, and Ryan gave it to the police. Tom Kuipers was arrested, and you're going to be officially cleared of all charges."

"What about jumping bail?" she asked. "I actually did that. I didn't show up for court when I was supposed to."

"For charges that never should have been pressed against you," he said. "We'll work it out. At the most, you'll get probation for that."

She released a ragged breath of relief. She wasn't going to have to give up their son and Jake. Jake...

Now she regretted that she'd stopped him from telling her how he felt about her. How did he feel about her?

"Can I get probation, too?" he asked.

And she stared at him. "I have no idea." How much trouble was he in for helping her elude the authorities? "Has anyone pressed charges against you for not bringing me in?"

He shook his head. "I'm asking for you to give me probation."

"I don't understand."

He took her hand in his and stroked his thumb across her knuckles. "I want you to give me a chance to prove to you that you can trust me, that I will never hurt you again."

"Oh, Jake..." Her heart swelled with all the love she felt for him. "You proved to me that I can trust you—when you risked your freedom and your life for me and our baby."

Jake was the kind of man on which Lillian could count—unlike her family. And his.

They had their own family now, though. So they didn't need to worry about their old ones.

"So you'll marry me?" he asked.

She tensed. "Why are you asking?" she wondered. "Because of the baby?"

"You said you could trust me now," Jake reminded her. "So trust that I love you and want to spend the rest of my life with you—even if we didn't have a child together."

"But we do," she said. "Are you all right with being a father?"

He sucked in a breath. "I'm scared," he admitted.

And that admission more than anything else proved himself worthy of her trust. He was being painfully honest and vulnerable with her.

"I don't know how to be a father," he said. "Mine wasn't a good one. He was abusive to my mother and to me."

She clutched both his hands in hers. "You are a loving and gentle man," she assured him. "You are nothing like your father."

"Just like you're nothing like your family," he said. "I used to think I couldn't trust you because of what they are. And I should have known better."

She sighed. "That makes two of us. I should have known better than to trust them."

"Donny came through for you," he said.

She snorted. "I know the O'Hanigans found him and forced the flash drive from him. He didn't willingly help me." She could understand why Jake had doubts about his ability to be a parent because of his family. At least she'd had her mother and grandmother to set examples for her on how to be loving and selfless.

"Once he turned over the flash drive, he didn't have to go with us to meet Kuipers," Jake said. "He knew it was going to be dangerous. But he insisted on coming along. And really, if you think about it, we wouldn't even be back together if he'd done what you asked."

Her happiness dimmed. "You wouldn't have sought me out if I hadn't jumped bail?"

He shook his head. "I wanted to call you, to talk to you. I missed you like crazy. But I thought you hated me and that you would never forgive me."

She'd thought that, too. And she'd tried to hate him when he'd come into her life again. But then he'd risked his own life to help her.

"So, really, we owe Donny," Jake persisted.

His defense of her brother surprised her, even as it proved that much further to her what a good man he was. And if any good had come out of her brother, she suspected that was because of Jake. Because his fearlessness and determination to risk his life to rescue her had inspired Donny to be a better man.

But he would never be Jake.

Nobody would.

He was one in a million. The love of her life.

"You don't deserve probation," she told him.

And he flinched.

So she continued, "You deserve life…" She leaned

forward and cupped his handsome face in her palms. Then she kissed his lips. "…with me."

He released a shaky breath. "You'll marry me?"

She nodded.

He arched a brow in skepticism and teased, "Because of the baby?"

She shook her head but added, "He needs a name. A first name and your last name." She ran her fingertips along Jake's strong jaw. She hoped the baby grew up to be as handsome as his father was. "And I would have told you that you were a father," she said. "I wouldn't have been able to keep him from you."

His brow arched even higher. "Even though you hated me?"

"I would have gotten over that," she said. "Because I love what we created together. Our son."

Jake grinned. "What do you want to call him? Davis? Donald?"

"Nothing with a *D*," she said with a shudder. "I want him to be his own person." And not judged because of who his family was.

Jake nodded in agreement. "You're right. How about Slate—and his life will be a clean one?"

She smiled. It was perfect. Just like Jake. "Slater, and Slate for short."

Jake smiled, too. But then the smile slid away. "So if not for Slater, why do you want to marry me, Lillian?"

She leaned forward and kissed him again. "I told you before…"

His brow puckered with confusion. "What? When?"

She hadn't even told him months ago that she

loved him—even though she'd felt it. She'd been waiting for him to say it first. When he hadn't and she'd found out he was a bounty hunter, she'd thought he hadn't cared about her at all. Now she knew better. She knew he loved her, too.

"Before I left to meet Mr. Kuipers."

"When I was passed out?" he asked.

Maybe she shouldn't have reminded him of what she had done—even though he claimed he'd already forgiven her. But had he really?

The way he looked at her, though, convinced her that he had. Because he was looking at her the same way he had looked at their son—with awe and love.

"I was scared to tell you when you were awake," she admitted. "In case you didn't feel the same way."

And the smile was back, curving his lips. "What way is that?"

"I love you, Jake. That's why I want to marry you," she admitted. "Not for our son."

But she was glad that he would have two loving, committed parents.

"But for me," she continued, "because I love you."

"I asked you to marry me," he said, "because I love you. And I want to spend the rest of my life proving that love to you. And I want that life—our life together—to start right now."

Donny didn't know what to say. Sorry was woefully inadequate. Hell, the honorable thing to do was to leave. But he'd wanted to see his nephew. And when Jake had caught him staring through the neonatal unit window at his son, he'd brought him back to Lillian's room.

"She won't want to see me," he protested.

"She's Lillian," Jake said. "She doesn't hold a grudge or she wouldn't have agreed to marry me."

His mouth dropped open in shock. "Really?"

"Yes." But Jake said it with wonder like he couldn't believe it, either.

Before Donny could congratulate him, Jake pushed open the door to Lillian's room and shoved Donny ahead of him.

She was sleeping, but when he stumbled forward, she opened her eyes. He expected to see hatred in them. After what he'd done, she had every reason to hate him. But she only looked at him as if she wasn't quite sure what she was seeing.

He wanted her to see him the way she once had— as someone she loved and trusted. But he would have to work to earn that back.

"I'm sorry," he said. "I know I let you down." His voice cracked as emotion overwhelmed him. He dropped to his knees next to the bed and pressed his head against the mattress. "I'm so, so sorry."

A hand stroked his head. "I know. I know you are."

It wasn't forgiveness. Not yet. But he couldn't ask that of her. Not after what he'd done. "I'll make it up to you," he vowed. "I promise. Whatever you want— free babysitting—"

"Give me away," she said.

"What?" He looked up and met her gaze.

Tears streamed from her eyes, too, but she was smiling. Her tears were happy ones. "Jake asked me to marry him. I want you to give me away at our wedding."

He glanced nervously at Jake then. He was surprised the guy hadn't already killed him. Jake Howard hadn't thought much of the Davies family to begin with; what Donny had done could have only made that opinion even worse.

But instead of glaring at him, Jake just nodded.

Maybe the doctors had given him some painkillers for his gunshot wound that had mellowed him.

"Are you sure you want me there?" Donny asked them both. "I wouldn't blame you if you never wanted to see me again."

If the situation was reversed, he would probably feel that way about her. But Lillian would never do what he'd done. She didn't have a selfish or self-serving bone in her body. She was as beautiful as their mother had been.

Donny felt a pang, missing their mother. And he knew he'd come close to losing Lillian, too.

"Jake is the one who pointed out to me that if you'd done what I'd asked you—"

"Delivered that flash drive to your lawyer," Donny finished for her.

"Then the charges would have been dropped."

Donny's stomach clenched with dread and misery. "I know."

"And Jake never would have come after me for jumping bail," she said.

Realization dawned on Donny. "And then the two of you never would have gotten back together." He'd never been a matchmaker before. He grinned. "That's good."

"That we never would have gotten back together?" Jake asked, and his voice was low and gruff now with anger and resentment and the risk of Donny dying at his hands.

"No, no," Donny quickly assured him. "Not at all! I'm happy you are." It was clear to him now how much the bounty hunter loved his sister—so much that he'd risked his life and taken a bullet for her.

Donny's little nephew was damn lucky he had Jake Howard for a father. And Lillian would be damn lucky to have him for a husband. It didn't matter to Donny anymore what his father thought about their relationship. What mattered was what was best for Lillian, and that was Jake.

"And I'd be happy to give you away," he said. He wasn't their father. And he was damn glad of that. He intended to be a better man than his father was.

He intended to be like Jake.

* * * * *

Get 4 FREE REWARDS!

We'll send you 2 FREE Books
plus 2 FREE Mystery Gifts.

Harlequin® Romantic Suspense books feature heart-racing sensuality and the promise of a sweeping romance set against the backdrop of suspense.

FREE
Value Over
$20

YES! Please send me 2 FREE Harlequin® Romantic Suspense novels and my 2 FREE gifts (gifts are worth about $10 retail). After receiving them, if I don't wish to receive any more books, I can return the shipping statement marked "cancel." If I don't cancel, I will receive 4 brand-new novels every month and be billed just $4.99 per book in the U.S. or $5.74 per book in Canada. That's a savings of at least 12% off the cover price! It's quite a bargain! Shipping and handling is just 50¢ per book in the U.S. and 75¢ per book in Canada*. I understand that accepting the 2 free books and gifts places me under no obligation to buy anything. I can always return a shipment and cancel at any time. The free books and gifts are mine to keep no matter what I decide.

240/340 HDN GMYZ

Name (please print)

Address   Apt. #

City   State/Province   Zip/Postal Code

Mail to the Reader Service:
IN U.S.A.: P.O. Box 1341, Buffalo, NY 14240-8531
IN CANADA: P.O. Box 603, Fort Erie, Ontario L2A 5X3

Want to try two free books from another series? Call 1-800-873-8635 or visit www.ReaderService.com.

---

*Terms and prices subject to change without notice. Prices do not include applicable taxes. Sales tax applicable in N.Y. Canadian residents will be charged applicable taxes. Offer not valid in Quebec. This offer is limited to one order per household. Books received may not be as shown. Not valid for current subscribers to Harlequin® Romantic Suspense books. All orders subject to approval. Credit or debit balances in a customer's account(s) may be offset by any other outstanding balance owed by or to the customer. Please allow 4 to 6 weeks for delivery. Offer available while quantities last.

Your Privacy—The Reader Service is committed to protecting your privacy. Our Privacy Policy is available online at www.ReaderService.com or upon request from the Reader Service. We make a portion of our mailing list available to reputable third parties that offer products we believe may interest you. If you prefer that we not exchange your name with third parties, or if you wish to clarify or modify your communication preferences, please visit us at www.ReaderService.com/consumerschoice or write to us at Reader Service Preference Service, P.O. Box 9062, Buffalo, NY 14240-9062. Include your complete name and address.

HRS18

"If I had someone to come home to, I might be more inclined not to burn the midnight oil."

The sound of Austin's voice and her desire for the same thing dropped on her like a ton of bricks. She glanced at him, but he was polishing off his Danish and didn't look at her. She couldn't read too much into those words. He was just talking.

"Jenna, I think we need to talk about this thing between us."

She set her empty cup on the tray with a thump. She stared at him for a moment. "I know. But I don't want to pick it apart, Austin. I feel something for you and you feel something for me."

"It's not that simple. I'm working on a case that directly involves your family member, we have a past and if my boss finds out I'm sleeping with you… Jesus." He ran his hand through his hair.

"We won't tell her, Austin. It's our business. Sure, we have a past, and we have some things we need to work through and figure out, but I want to do that. You have a life in San Diego and I have one in DC. We have limited time together—do we have to be rational and serious?"

His expression changing again, he reached down and cupped her jaw, running his thumb along her bottom lip. His eyes were dark and shadowed, but she could see the hunger in them. "I'm a realist," he said, his voice gruff. He caressed her mouth again. "I understand what you want to do, but we'll have to face whatever comes. I just don't want to be blindsided, and I don't want to freaking take advantage of you."

She couldn't help but smile through this serious conversation. "Were you there this morning when I seduced you?"

He released a breath on a half laugh. "Right, and, lady, you did a thorough job of it." He caressed her cheek with his thumb. "I'm serious about this. I don't want to hurt you, and I'm not keen on getting hurt."

"I don't want that, either. But can't we just enjoy this for as long as we can? Save the big decisions for later?"

He closed his eyes and pulled her close. She slid her arm around his waist, and her eyes burned as he caught her up in a fierce hold, his face turned against hers. "All right. I'm apparently weak when it comes to you. I can't resist this...or you," he whispered.

She wanted time with him to discover exactly what had driven them apart six years ago. But a little voice whispered in her head, *You're afraid*, as the wind whipped up into a frenzy and blew hard and hot against the complex. She shivered and he drew the covers up over her shoulders.

Or maybe it was because she might discover something she couldn't live without.

Don't miss
AGENT BODYGUARD by Karen Anders,
available July 2018 wherever
Harlequin® Romantic Suspense books and ebooks are sold.

www.Harlequin.com

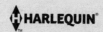

ROMANTIC suspense

Heart-racing romance, breathless suspense

Don't miss the thrilling TOP SECRET DELIVERIES miniseries!

Available July 2018

These heroes will do anything to protect their families and the women they love!

www.Harlequin.com

LOVE
Harlequin romance?

Join our Harlequin community to share your thoughts and connect with other romance readers!

Be the first to find out about promotions, news, and exclusive content!

Sign up for the Harlequin e-newsletter and download a free book from any series at
www.TryHarlequin.com

CONNECT WITH US AT:

Harlequin.com/Community

 Facebook.com/HarlequinBooks

 Twitter.com/HarlequinBooks

 Instagram.com/HarlequinBooks

Pinterest.com/HarlequinBooks

ReaderService.com

 HARLEQUIN®

**ROMANCE WHEN
YOU NEED IT**

HSOCIAL2017